I gazed in
pink lips seemed at home here. It made no sense. I
knew this. I hadn't been away from society for so long
that I couldn't see the absurdity of the situation. And
yet, this soft head, full of downy silken tresses, so
different from my son's, had nestled into me. Tears
silently streamed down my face at just the thought of
him. A life snatched away at birth.

Even in the blink of an eye between his birth and
burial, I'd memorized his milky scent, the swirl of dark
hair, his almond hooded eyes. A stray tear plunks onto
this baby's head. I quickly wiped it away and watched
the child ravenously gulp until slumber took over.

Had I really just nursed a child that I found on my
doorstep? And now what? Call the police? Tell them
that I just happened to birth my own child, at home a
few days ago? That I just happened to bury his small
form in my yard? I just happened to find a new child,
and decided to keep it for myself?

It was beyond absurd. I had not even yet filled out
a birth certificate. A death certificate. Not to mention
that I buried my son myself. Wasn't that illegal? And
what would come of this baby?

Foster care? It was a sentence almost as bad as
death. I should know. I had lived it.

Praise for *Choosing Charity,* by Sara Zavacki-Moore

"This is a story of flawed people trying to figure out how to make the most of life when difficult curveballs keep getting thrown at them. They're difficult, they're numb, they're manic, they're desperate, they're codependent. And it's all done in a way I would consider respectful."

~ Evelyn Silver, Witch's Knight

"Choosing Charity is an insightful and poignant story about the daily struggle of life and relationships.. Prepare for a roller-coaster of emotion that will leave you with a whole new perspective on mental illness."

~ Jennifer Peer, The Last Bloom

"A story of sacrifice, self-discovery, and the search for love."

~ Joanne Brokaw, *Suddenly Stardust*

"What follows is at times amusing, often profound, and generally reflective of feelings not often recognized or expressed. I was pulled in with the first sentence."

~ L. VanNostrand, M.S.in Child Development

Tiny House of God

by

Sara Zavacki-Moore

Tiny House of God

Cover Art by *Kim Mendoza*

The Wild Rose Press, Inc.
PO Box 708
Adams Basin, NY 14410-0708
Visit us at www.thewildrosepress.com

Publishing History
First Edition, 2023
Trade Paperback ISBN 978-1-5092-4849-0
Digital ISBN 978-1-5092-4850-6

Published in the United States of America

Dedication

To Lydia, I am so proud of you. You are amazing. Your brilliance, creativity, kindness, and insight will continue to touch the lives of those around you. Keep shining, sharing, and creating.
To Malcolm, You see more than most. Keep looking.
To Matt, You love harder than anyone I know. Keep loving.
I love you all.
You are my church.

Acknowledgments

I once had a friend who likened writing a book to the birth of a child. Having birthed two of my own, I can honestly say that birth was much more painful. However, much of my material did have great moments of pain that would often leave me breathless or crying.

Writing is a journey. For some, it is an escape to a beautiful fantasy world, for others it's an adventure filled with triumph. For me, it is a form of therapy. As a therapist and a survivor of trauma (aren't we all?)I have had the privilege of sitting with many people in pain. I am honored to be trusted enough to share in their journeys.

Thank you to the Rochester Religious Society of Friends (Quakers) for offering me a safe space to silently listen for the voice of a loving God.

Thank you Reading Between the Wines book club for your friendship and support.

A special thank you to my dearest friends, Rachel, Sylvia & Danielle for being my Aubrey.

This second novel has also been a journey, one which I couldn't have taken without the help and support of many lovely people. If I have neglected to name you, I apologize. My ineptitude is not intentional.

First, thank you to my wonderful editor and friend, Melanie Billings. I am forever grateful to you for believing in me, and for helping my dream of publishing happen (twice!)

Thank you to my strongest ally and first reader, Matthew Moore. I couldn't ask for a better partner to journey through this life with. Your feedback helped me reshape the book into something I am even more proud of.

Thank you to my beta reader extraordinaire, Laura Vanessa Normandy. Your thoughtful suggestions and keen eye helped make this book so much better.

Thank you to my cover artists, Kim Mendoza and RJ Morris, as well as the cover artist for Choosing Charity, Debbie Taylor. You both brought my vision to light. I am so grateful for your time and talent.

A special thank you to the kind beta reader for Choosing Charity, Flo Hicks. I am so sorry that I forgot to add your name last time around.

Thank you to fellow authors, Joanne Brokaw, Jen Peer and Evelyn Silver for your encouragement and reviews.

Thank you to the Wild Rose Press, especially to Rhonda Penders. Your kindness, support and generosity go above and beyond. I am blessed to be a part of The Wild Rose Press garden!

Lastly, I want to thank all of the friends, family, and strangers who have been kind enough to follow me on social media, purchase my books, leave reviews and encourage me. I am so very grateful for this opportunity to turn my pain into art. I encourage each of you to do the same.

Don't let them in.
Don't let them know.
Keep them at bay.
Not friend,
but foe.

Prologue

June 5, 1991

Metal scraped and screamed against the soft summer sunlight. The jaws of life ripped open the decimated hood to release my mother from the crushed dashboard of the car. Her swollen belly jutted out beneath the strained seatbelt. Spider veined and crackled; the windshield cupped her bloodstained face. My grandmother's unconscious form draped across the steering wheel as the bus she crashed into opened its unharmed doors to release the passengers now stunned into silence. They watched in horror as emergency workers struggled to remove my family from the wreckage.

Teetering between realms, I watched the shallow rise and fall of my mother's chest. My temporary dwelling was crumbling. It was three months too soon for my arrival.

"Go." My grandmother urged me forward. Her voice carried away in the sultry wind.

"I'm sorry," my mother whispered into my still-developing ears as her soul joined her mother's, and they continued their journey into the next life without me.

Welcome to the world, baby girl.
You are an abandoned miracle.

Chapter One

August 21, 2020

The howling baby abandoned on my front step quieted as soon as I opened the door. I stood for a moment in frozen silence. *Am I imagining this?* Glancing around my neatly tended front yard, I saw no other clues as to how this child had arrived. A few scuffle marks were left in the dirt, perhaps, but nothing else seemed out of the ordinary.

As I crouched down to get a closer look, the baby hiccupped and began to cry again. As if on cue, my swollen breasts began to leak. Tingly shocks of electricity gave way to nature's call. Life was cruel. Was this a joke? A delusion? I looked down at my now milk-soaked T-shirt, confirming that I was indeed awake. Just a few short days ago, I had given birth. A son. A prank that God had played on me. A moment of glory, only to be snatched away. I had buried him myself. My bloated, swollen body had moved slowly. The shovel held tight in my hand as I blindly dug at the earth. My tears watered the soil as I placed his small, bundled form in the midst of my rose garden.

I awoke this morning feeling as though my breasts had turned to stone. No one warned me that your milk keeps coming even after your baby is gone.

Snapping out of my haze, I eased myself to the

ground next to the box. A baby in a box. This can't be. I must be imagining it or dreaming. I reached down, tucking my fingers behind the child, lifting him gently. Was it a boy? The pastel, elephant-printed fleece provided me with no clue. I rose awkwardly, my body still weak and sore. I nestled the child onto my shoulder as he or she continued to cry. My breasts were still somehow aching and dripping. Only yesterday, I had frantically dug out the breast pump I'd been given at my shower. It was still wrapped in golden paper tied with pink and blue ribbon. Without even washing the apparatus, I pulled out the enclosed pamphlet and followed the directions as I sobbed in relief. Within a few painful moments, each of the pump's bottles were full. I dumped the contents onto the rose bushes. It seemed a waste to simply drain the liquid gold down the sink.

Quickly, I carried the child into the house. Then, thinking twice, I stepped back outside to pull the box in as well. Easing the door shut, I clicked the lock in place and pushed the box with my foot as we made our way to the couch. Gently laying the child down, I regarded the small bundle. The baby was swaddled in two light blankets. A few extra folded blankets, five diapers, and a container of wipes had been placed under the child. The baby regarded me silently. I stared back, knowing exactly what it was that I wanted to do. I looked down into this tiny face and lifted the child to my breast.

Sweet relief flooded my system as my milk let down. I gazed in wonder at this foreign child whose tiny pink lips seemed at home here. It made no sense. I knew this. I hadn't been away from society for so long that I couldn't see the absurdity of the situation. And yet, this soft head, full of downy silken tresses, so different from my son's, had nestled into me. Tears silently streamed down my face at just the thought of him. *A life snatched away at birth. That's all God would give me. Why even give me that, just to take it from me? Allowing me to see the beauty of a life that cannot be?*

Even in the blink of any eye between his birth and burial, I'd memorized his milky scent, the swirl of dark hair, his almond hooded eyes. A stray tear plunks onto this baby's head. I quickly wiped it away and watched the child ravenously gulp until slumber took over.

Eventually, I eased the sleeping child off of me. Placing the warm bundle on the couch, I studied the scrunched-up face. *Had I really just nursed a child that I found on my doorstep? And now what? Call the police? Tell them that I just happened to birth my own child at home a few days ago? That I just happened to bury his small form in my yard? I just happened to find a new child and decided to keep it for myself?*

It was beyond absurd. I had not even yet filled out a birth certificate. A death certificate. *Not to mention that I buried my son myself. Wasn't that illegal? And what would come of this baby? Foster care?* It was a sentence almost as bad as death. I should know. I had lived it.

****

To: Melaniewalker@catharsistimepress.com
From:Willowmorgan666@gmail.com
Subject: title to be determined: AGE 6
Mel, Here's the next chapter, as requested. Please let me know if there is anything you want me to edit or revise. I'm already working on the next section for the

book and will get it to you before the publisher's deadline. Thanks, -W.

My first day in foster care was the last day I saw my father. Isn't it ironic that no matter how neglectful or abusive a parent is, their child can still love them? I remember screaming for him as the social worker calmly tried to take me away. Why would I have wanted to stay? I was filthy, hungry, and covered in red, itchy bumps. I can still recall the satisfaction I derived from scratching my skin so raw that it bled. The tip of my right shoulder still bears the scars of some of the damage I did. That scar is right next to the one my father gave me with the butt of his cigarette. I had asked for food one too many times. I'd awakened him from his drunken stupor trying to sneak spare change from his coat pocket so I could walk down to the corner store. Why didn't I think to remove his coat from the back of the filthy kitchen chair before rummaging through his pockets? If only I had thought of that. But I was only five.

We did have some food. Cans lined the dusty shelves in the basement. Dented, expired cans. So many cans, but no opener. The last time I asked for the opener, my father laughed at me. He'd awakened long enough to laugh at my neediness, to offer me a swig of his amber-colored liquid, and then to promptly pass out again. That was one of many nights I crawled under my blankets and went to sleep in order not to feel the familiar pangs of hunger. Only that night, my slumber was interrupted by the pounding on the door. Pounding he slept through. Relentless pounding that didn't stop until I'd opened the door to see a police officer and a large wild-haired woman on my porch. It hadn't taken them long to walk through our tiny apartment. To look in the fridge full of rotting food. To see the red bumps peeking out beneath my too-short pants. They spoke kindly to me. The wild-haired woman pulled a granola bar out of her coat pocket and offered it to me. She let me proudly show off my doll, Sally-baby. I had dressed her in my old baby clothes. The ones I found in an old box in the basement. She let me bring her with us as she packed me into the backseat of her rusty car. I held Sally-baby tight as I screamed for my father. I screamed even though I knew he could no longer hear me. The last time he woke up was yesterday when he'd laughed at me. His yellow eyes had only opened long enough to mock me. But I screamed for him anyway.

What is it people say about the correlation between a father figure and our view of God? That if you had a *bad* or absent father, it might make it hard to believe in a God of love? Maybe that was my problem. I never gave up on believing in God.

I just gave up on the love part.

****

August 21, 2020

My tiny living room floor was a mess. An unknown baby was asleep on my small couch, surrounded by handmade decorative throw pillows. The box now lay upturned on the rug. Besides the swaddled gift, there had been no other clues to make sense of this mystery. It was simply a diaper box. Its cardboard walls flaunted a huge glossy photo of a smiling baby. In addition to the child, there had been a small stack of neatly folded baby blankets, a few diapers, and some wipes underneath her. *Her or him?* I hadn't yet worked up the nerve to check. The multi-colored blankets hadn't offered me a clue as to the gender, each pastel print reminiscent of the wrapping paper I had opened at my own baby shower.

That shower seemed to be a lifetime ago. It was right before the pandemic hit. Back when we still met face-to-face. When the air didn't pose a toxic threat to humanity. Before Covid 19 changed our world forever.

My shower had been planned for the same day I was to move away. Just four short months ago, life had been so vastly different. I had a job; granted, it was with a temp agency, but it was work. My co-workers were generous with their gifts. Perhaps it was related to their guilt over never really getting to know me. That was all right with me. Getting to know each other wasn't high on my list of priorities. My plan had always been to take temp jobs and set aside enough money to have my tiny house built. It wasn't nearly as hard as I thought it would be. After all, I knew the *system*, and I was finally able to make it work to my advantage. Living in transitional housing was far from glamorous, but no one at my job knew about that. So, when the time came, I loaded my baby loot into my car, and headed for my little slice of country heaven.

Disappearing is easy. Live frugally. Save every penny you can. And have a parent or two die on you. My mother died in childbirth. So, I guess I missed out on all the maternal bonding stuff everyone raves about. It seemed as though I was bound for tragedy from the beginning. I'm told that my father fell apart after her death. Left with a newborn and a bottle of whiskey. I can't really recall much about my first few years of life. Apparently, most of us can only recollect a snippet or two of murky moments. I have flashes of memories.

Memories imprinted on my brain and stored in my body.

Once I had a social worker tell me my life would make a good made-for-television movie.

I still have no idea what she meant. I was never allowed to watch many movies. In fact, watching TV was a privilege that I rarely earned. By the time I was in my third, and least favorite, foster home, I had developed quite the appetite for TV. My first two foster families relied heavily on it. I fell in love with the cheesy re-runs featuring happy, achromatic families with moms and dads who thought their kids were angels from heaven. It was easy to plop down in front of the boxed god and worship. My revival services were cut short when I turned ten and moved in with the Calkins.

Chapter Two

*Mel, Here's another section. My therapist is happy
I'm working with you on this project. She's big into
expressive writing and was as excited as I've ever seen
her uber calm-hippy self when I told her that I was
offered this book deal. She keeps telling me how healing
this whole thing is going to be. I'm not so sure. I just
feel raw and exhausted. Anyway, here you go. Let me
know what you think. Thanks. -W*

At first, the Calkins family seemed nice enough.
As we pulled up to their two-story house in the city, my
case worker gasped. Both of the parents and all five of
their kids were standing on the front lawn waiting for
me. The kids were literally lined up in order of height,
like a ghetto version of the Von Trapp family. They
greeted me warmly, but I could tell from the look in
each one of their eyes that this was not a happy place to
be.

My caseworker, Angel, and yes, that was her real
name, had been so excited to bring me to this family on
my actual birthday. I had gotten so used to not
celebrating my birthday that it brought tears to my eyes
to see these strangers on their front lawn holding
homemade birthday signs for me. The littlest child, a

tiny girl with uneven pigtails, was even holding a helium balloon.

"Welcome home, Willow!"

The mother placed an absurd amount of emphasis on the word "home." She rushed over to the car door and opened it for me, reaching in to grab my hands and tug me out.

"Let me introduce you to everyone. I'm Mrs. Calkins, of course."

She then pointed to her husband, "This is Mr. Calkins, but you can call us mom and dad when you are ready."

She laughed as if it was silly of me to not want to call them that right away.

"Girls, come over here and introduce yourself to Willow."

Four well-dressed girls stepped forward. The tallest one, whose eyes were lined with thick black kohl, started.

"I'm Michelle. This is Tara and Kara." She pointed to the identical pair. "And that's Molly."

The twins stood there awkwardly, holding their multi-colored signs. One of them seemed to be smirking at me, while the other seemed to be studying the ground in front of her.

"Shell! I was gonna tell her my name! Not you. I wanted to do it!" Molly shuffled close to me, handing me the balloon.

"I'm Molly. I'm seven." She smiled, showing off her crooked incisor. "You are sharing a room with me!" Before I knew what was happening, she had wrapped her skinny arms around me and was squeezing me tight.

"Molly! What did I say about personal space?"

admonished Mrs. Calkins. She shook her head in disapproval as she pulled Molly from me. The tiny warmth momentarily around my middle was snatched away.

"Well," Angel cleared her throat. "Shall we go in and get you settled?" She lifted my plastic bag out of the backseat and closed the door. "I don't mean to rush things, but I have a meeting to get to."

"Of course, of course. Come in. Dillon, be a gentleman and get Willow's bag." The mother's voice sounded syrupy-sweet, yet her eyes looked sour. I watched as the only boy came over to me and silently took my bag. One side of his greasy, dark hair reached the tip of his shoulder. The other side was shaved, giving him the look of a miniature, damaged rock star. I immediately liked him.

"Thank you," I whispered as he peered at me from under his hair.

He gave me a small nod, then turned toward the house. As I climbed the steps up the porch, Molly planted herself beside me.

"I'll show you our room." The screen door slammed shut behind us. I froze for a moment. The grownups were still outside. I assumed they were busy talking about me. The twins had disappeared, and only Dillon and Molly seemed to care I was there. Obediently, I followed them through the living room full of mismatched furniture. The light brown couch was mostly covered with a large multicolored afghan. In front of the couch, a sturdy-looking coffee table held the biggest book I had ever seen. Molly caught me looking.

"Oh, that's Dad's special Bible. Whatever you do,

don't touch it. Come on!"

She pulled me toward the stairs. We followed Dillon up the wooden staircase, past the framed photos of strangers lining the walls. Sometimes the houses that look the nicest turn out to be the meanest.

****

I'd heard stories from the twins about their caseworker. At first, I thought they must have been exaggerating. By the time I met the girls, they'd already had nine different caseworkers. They couldn't even remember the newest one's name. But they were eager to describe her.

"She is super ugly, and she smells like egg salad." Tara chomped on her gum as she filled me in.

"No, more like yogurt." Kara held her hand out, palm up.

Tara sighed and pulled the gum out of her mouth to place it in Kara's hand.

For a moment, I thought she was going to put it in her own mouth.

"I told you to stop chewing this stupid stuff." Throwing it in the garbage, Kara picked up the retainer case from the dresser top and passed it to her sister. "And it's yogurt. She smells like yogurt. Plus, I swear she wears a wig."

"It's not a wig, Tara. If she was wearing a wig, why in the world would she pick a wig like that? Why would she pick such an ugly one? I mean, the color alone is gross. It's like dirty snow…like, sludge. That murky, dirty brown color, ugh, it's so ugly!"

Kara was only two minutes older than her sister, but she acted like she was her mother. Her bossiness drove me crazy. Most of the time, it was just easier to let her think she was in charge of all of us. Questioning her authority would result in lengthy debates with her, often ending with her somehow getting her way. Lucky for me, she focused most of her attention on Tara.

"Anyway, I am positive it's a wig. I saw her adjust it in the mirror the last time she was here. You know I'm right." Kara stood with her hand on her hip, shifting her eyes back and forth to Tara and me. Tara popped her retainer in.

"Whatever." She sighed.

****

August 21, 2022

The baby slumbered peacefully while I had a panic attack. *Breathe, Willow. Calm down.* I paced my tiny living room as I inhaled deeply, forcing my breath to slow down, seeking out my favorite items in the room, fingers grazing each one as I named them aloud.

"Blue bowl, stolen from the thrift store. Afghan from Angel. Ugly vase I made in the psych ward, photo from Molly." Standing in front of the photo, I traced along the outside of the popsicle frame with trembling fingers. *My dear Molly. The only one who truly got me. My kindred spirit.*

The photo was taken a few years after moving in with the Calkins. By then, I was in the awkward teenage phase. Gangly arms and legs, acne along my brow. My hair had lightened a bit from the many hours we spent outside that summer. Molly's fair skin was dotted with freckles. She hated those freckles, always complaining about them, but I loved them. They made her hazel eyes stand out even more. Sometimes at night, when she climbed into my bed, she would close her eyes and let me trace the constellations across her face.

Although she was nearly three years younger than me, I preferred her company to that of the twins or Dillon. By then, Michelle had aged out of the system and was long gone. Letting me share a room with Molly was the kindest thing the Calkins did.

Shrill cries woke me from my daydream. Kneeling down, I placed my hand on the bundled child. Scooping the baby up, I made my way to the nook under my stairs, where my own baby's bassinet lay empty. I placed the child down on the blue and white fabric and began to change its diaper. A girl. The newborn diapers were snug, but I made it work. She stared at me while I looked down at her and cried.

"What do I do with you?" I shook my head. "What will people think?" *What people? Actually, who would know?* I didn't really have any friends at this point. I mean, I had online friends who would periodically check on me. But I hadn't been on social media much since Charles had sent me a friend request. He was my first and last one-night stand. I had no desire to have him in my life. *Maybe this is all a dream? A delusion of sorts? Some type of postpartum thing?*

I ran back through the living room and out the front door. Circling around to the backyard, I approached the tiny clearing among my rose bushes. Kneeling down on the freshly dug earth, I placed both hands on top of the large smooth rock I had placed there. He was still there. Right where I left him. Under the loosened earth.

Cicadas buzzed as a slight breeze blew at the damp hair at the nape of my neck. My hands began turning white from pressing down on the rock. Hadn't I already cried all of my tears? No, apparently not. I moved my hands aside and lay my cheek on the cold, hard surface.

How can it hurt so much to miss something I barely had?

Closing my eyes, I could see his sweet little face. Feel the slight weight of his body against my chest. *I did everything right. I followed all the rules. No smoking or drinking, no lunch meat or soft cheese…. I even took those huge vitamins every single day. Social distancing before it was mandated. Disinfecting every grocery before putting it away. And, what good had it done? True, I lucked out by not getting Covid yet, but I still couldn't manage to save my own child.*

When I had bored God with my cursing and crying, I wiped my face with my sleeve, picked myself up, and walked back around to the front of my house. I'd already left the child inside unattended for far too long. Perhaps I really wasn't good mother material.

The piece of land I'd been given was vast, and despite all of my lamenting over the past few days, no one was even remotely close enough to hear me.

By some miracle, my father had opened some sort of special savings account for me shortly after I was born. He'd also managed to write up a will in the midst of his bingeing, leaving me a chunk of money to inherit when I turned twenty-five. That was the year I started looking into tiny houses. It was so much easier than I thought it would be. Turns out there are a lot of options for buying or even building a tiny house. I found an older model that a retired couple up in Canada had built about ten years ago. When they decided to create a fully accessible home without an upper loft, they put their tiny house up for sale. It wasn't fancy, and it needed a bit of work, but after taking a trip up North to see it, I knew it was just right for me. So, while they built their new place, I stayed in cheap transitional housing that Angel found for me. I worked at the temp agency, saving away as much money as possible. Two short years later, I paid a boatload of money to have my new home relocated here. After depleting most of my savings, I finally had a place to call my own.

****

I studied the ground where I had found the baby. There was no logic to it. Who would leave a baby in front of a tiny house in the middle of nowhere? *During a pandemic? And* why *my* tiny house? Did this person know that *I* had been pregnant? That *I* couldn't even manage to keep my own baby alive? And so, they left one in his place? I stared down at my hands, counting all ten fingers, slowing my breathing down with each number I repeated in my head. As baffling as it was, this was not a lucid dream. Bewildered, I slowly climbed the front step, walked inside, and quietly closed the door.

Returning to the alcove and peeking over the side of the bassinet, I saw she was again sleeping peacefully. In a daze, I moved to the center of my living room. There was comfort in the fact that I could see both ends of my house from any position. There were no scary hallways or haunted basements, no spaces in which someone could be hiding. Each item, every piece of furniture, was carefully selected. I had everything I needed. My handmade sofa took up the majority of the living room. I built it myself after watching countless video tutorials. I guess the time I spent as a kid volunteering for *Carpentry for Christ* must have left me with a few skills, not to mention a handful of scars. It wasn't pretty, but it fit perfectly. I couldn't figure out how to make something fancier, perhaps something that converted to a daybed. However, I managed to build three pull-out drawers underneath. I'd even sewn the blue denim cushions. I made them by hand after giving up on trying to figure out how to work the sewing machine I got at a flea market. It was one of those old heavy wooden and metal sewing machines. The kind that was a legit piece of antique furniture. It now stood retired by the end of my sofa, a slide-out wooden shelf serving as a make-shift desk. More often than not, I used it to eat my frozen dinners there each night.

The walls were painted a light yellow, with white trim throughout the interior. A few feet away from the sofa was my kitchen area. My two- burner stove and copper sink butted up against the apartment-sized refrigerator. Its white doors are marred by only one magnet, a gift from Angel. She had given it to me on my eighteenth birthday, the day I was no longer officially on her caseload. The magnet was beautiful. It was made of twisted, multi-colored metal strips fashioned to spell out my favorite word: *Freedom.*

At the edge of the kitchen, there was a sliding wooden pocket door, also painted white. Beyond the door was the bathroom. The space was so small I could barely fit in there when I was bloated and pregnant. A simple half sink, toilet, and stand-up shower with a deep copper sitting tub along the bottom made it nearly impossible to kneel down in front of the actual toilet to throw up. And I had done a lot of throwing up while pregnant. I was sick until the week before my son was born, in fact. It had gotten so difficult to try kneeling in front of the toilet, I had taken to just going outside and throwing up.

The actual land was owned by my uncle. Honestly, I think he offered it to me in a fit of guilt over his absence in my life. One of the things that bothered me the most about foster care was that I hadn't necessarily needed to grow up in the system. Yet, even after his own brother died, my uncle was too busy with his own life to become a part of mine. The smiling faces of his golden-haired daughters, my cousins, filled his social media posts. Flaunting family celebrations that never included me. Outside of making me feel bad for having a less than glossy life, having online relationships did come in handy. After posting that I was looking for land for my tiny house, my uncle responded right away. He offered me an acre on the edge of his property. Free of charge. I didn't feel the least bit guilty accepting it. He even made it possible to plug into his electricity and water until I saved up enough money to become fully *off-grid*.

The very edge of my wooden kitchen counter also served as a step. Two smaller steps led to the actual counter. Above the counter were three additional steps leading to my loft. Underneath each step, drawers were installed for additional storage. Since I never really had many possessions to my name, a few of the drawers remain empty. The rest are used for my clothing, shoes, backpack, and even extra food.

My sleeping loft consisted of a queen sized mattress and a floating bedside table with a lamp on it. If I sat up in bed, my head almost touched the ceiling. Two circular windows graced each side of the upper walls, along with a small skylight. The skylight was by far my favorite part of the tiny house. It made my bedroom area feel both cozy and light, and I relished stretching out on my mattress and gazing at the stars. Plus, the skylight could be fully opened, allowing me to escape onto the roof if needed. Someday, I would love to build a small fence up there so I could do yoga on my roof. Maybe even create a rooftop garden.

Having a comfortable and clean place to sleep was a luxury that I wasn't afforded much as a child. My first foster home was especially filthy. Bags of garbage stayed tied up by the back door for days, sometimes weeks. Roaches were frequent house guests. And I swear that the paltry carpet in the living room had some type of fungus growing in it. I once pulled a white mushroomy thing from the horrid rug. But compared to the living conditions with my father, all of those foster homes were sparkling clean. After living with what I later learned to be bedbugs, I was relieved to be rid of the perpetual itchiness I had grown accustomed to.

Chapter Three

To: Melaniewalker@catharsistimepress.com
From:Willowmorgan666@gmail.com
Subject: Age 14
I beat the deadline! Here ya go. -W

The Calkins prided themselves on just how clean their house looked. Everything was old and used, but Mrs. C often lectured us about cleanliness being next to godliness. The six of us were given a list of daily chores to do around the house. And even though everything was basically cleaned daily, she would make us do the same chores again the next day anyway. To her, daily chores were the eleventh commandment. And Commandments were the first thing I learned while living there.

Despite being a clean place to live, I hated it. The one saving grace was sharing a room with Molly. No matter how difficult my day had been, every night after we had all been told to go to sleep, Molly would quietly climb out of her bed and into mine. Her small body was toasty warm against my side. We would wait until the house was silent and still and whisper about our futures. Eventually, our conversation would slow, replacing daydreams with light snores. Somehow, each morning when I woke, Molly would be back in her bed. She was scared Mrs. C would find out and be mad. The one time she had been caught asleep in my bed, we had awakened to Mrs. C stomping in the room, turning the light switch on and off rapidly and yanking the covers off of us. Jarred out of our slumber, we both immediately sat up. Before I could even say anything, Mrs. C had grabbed Molly by the arm, pulling her off my bed and flinging her onto her own.

"Beds are not for sharing." Spittle flew from Mrs. C pursed lips as she berated us.

"The only bed to share is the marriage bed!" Crossing the room and easing the Bible from our bookshelf, she opened it, mumbling as she flipped through its thin pages. Clearing her throat, she looked me straight in the eye before glancing back down.

"First Thessalonians, chapter 5, verses 21 and 22, 'Prove all things; hold fast that which is good. Abstain from all appearance of evil.'"

After reading, she slammed the book closed. Before turning to leave, she stared at us suspiciously before speaking through gritted teeth,

"Don't let me see this happen again, or you will both be spanked." Her words spit out with fury.

Spanking was a regular occurrence in the Calkins' house. Mr. Calkins was the disciplinarian. He kept a large leather belt hanging on the wall outside of the upstairs bedroom. Often, Mrs. Calkins would tell us calmly ahead of time that we were to go upstairs for our father to discipline us. It seemed as though any type of behavior was spank-worthy. Slamming doors, stomping up the stairs, talking back, or complaining about chores were all considered sins. Of course, any of these offenses also warranted a Biblical lecture.

"I'm only doing this to teach you a lesson about obedience," he would say. *Spare the rod, spoil the child,* was the family motto. Mrs. C had even made a colorful framed cross stitch of the phrase and placed it on the wall in the upstairs hallway.

"God has put me in a position of authority over you," Mr. C would continue while standing over me. "You are to obey authority at all times. I am obeying God's instructions to raise you up in accordance with His laws." Mr. C obeyed God's instructions on the matter until I was fourteen, and I finally worked up the nerve to approach Mrs. C about it. She terrified me with her sappy sweet voice and her devilish glare. Hesitantly, I approached her one day while she was folding laundry and placing it on top of the dryer.

"Excuse me, Mrs. C?" I mumbled.

"You mean, mom? She would draw out the sound of each letter, waiting for me to respond.

"Yes, um, mom. Um, I was wondering if, um…if instead of being spanked, another type of discipline can be used?

"What are you talking about?" She paused in her folding to study me.

"Well, it's just that, the last time I got a spanking, I uh, I had my period, and it was kind of awkward." I kept my eyes locked on the patterned linoleum.

"I see. Yes, I guess that makes sense. I will talk with your father." She stared out the window at the backyard. When I remained silent, she turned back to me and cleared her throat.

"I will take care of it." I raised my eyes to see if I had permission to leave the room. She gave me a small nod, and I gratefully escaped.

Thankfully, I was never spanked again.

****

June 30, 2020

Life in my tiny house was peaceful. I rarely felt lonely. After a lifetime of being forced to live with people I didn't like, being on my own was blissful. Wi-Fi was my biggest luxury, and I relished being able to reach out to the few friends that I did have if I wanted to. I'd lucked out by finding a few online writing projects to supplement my income and relied heavily on having internet access for ordering my groceries and other household items. If the power went out, I would be forced to return to the real world. After leaving my temp job to move here, I had only heard from a few people. Angel had offered to come over to help me unpack. Since I knew how busy her schedule was, I turned her down. My friend Kristy from my old job still messaged me about once a week. If I waited more than a few hours to reply to her, she would begin stalking me down through all of my social media platforms.

After the first week in my new place, I learned my lesson. Initially, Kristy messaged me early one morning. I ignored the additional three messages from her as I was busy working on my garden. By the time I had come in for lunch, she had left me several voicemail messages. Before risking her actually showing up at my house, I called her back around two p.m.

"Willow, what the hell? I've been calling you all day. Are you okay? Are you in labor?" Kristy's nasally upstate voice made her sound angry, even when she wasn't.

"I'm *fine*. No, I'm not in labor. I have like three months before I'm due." I laughed.

"Yeah, I know—but there is such a thing as preterm labor." Kristy had no children of her own, but was more well-versed in pregnancy and childbirth than anyone I knew. She practically begged me to allow her to be present for the birth. So, when I lied and told her I was considering a home birth, with only a doula or midwife present, she was clearly disappointed. I placated her by asking her to send me research on home births. She considered herself a research queen, and I figured it would make her feel involved in some way.

"Well, I just wanted to make sure you were okay. I know you are all alone." She interrupted my thoughts.

"You say that as if it's a bad thing. I like being alone." I reminded her. "That's why I moved out here." Technically, I wasn't too far away from the city. My uncle's property was in a small western suburb, only about forty minutes from downtown. When people hear I'm from New York, they automatically think I live in New York City. In reality, I live in Western NY, closer to Buffalo. It's about seven hours away from NYC, and unlike the city, it is beautiful. Hiltville is a cozy village, mostly consisting of farms and country homes. There is a small main street area that hosts the school, post-office, fire & police departments, and a few stores and restaurants. My property is out in the country, but only about a ten-minute drive to the little main street.

I grew up in what many would consider the ghetto. All three of the foster homes I lived in were in the city. One of the strange things about this area is the disparity of wealth. It's even worse now. Some of my old neighborhoods are now posh, full of new luxury high-rises, independent theaters, and fancy cafes. Yet, drive down a few blocks, and you will be in the poorest areas of the city. Sometimes one end of a street will be well-tended, with beautiful houses and manicured lawns, while the other end is full of boarded-up crack houses and a corner store that is littered with homeless people and drug dealers. Even back then, multiple shootings were a daily part of life, and just standing outside at the bus stop was a risk.

I grew up on the wrong end of the street. My neighborhood consisted of huge old houses that were converted into multiple-family apartments. Often, these homes were owned by slumlords, some of whom didn't even live in NY. Our rent was mostly paid by the Department of Social Services through a voucher. Since the landlord had a steady source of monthly income through DSS, there was little incentive for them to take good care of the property. When I think back on the amount of money my foster parents must have been making off of us kids, the poverty made no sense. It wasn't until years later I found out that Molly and I were the only kids they were actually getting paid for. The twins and Dillon were technically relatives, and some loophole prevented them from getting proper funding from the state. Molly and I always speculated Mr. Calkins was squirreling money away somewhere, but given the number of lectures about tithing to the church, it seemed most likely the money that should have been spent on us was being given directly to his obsession. The price of admission to a future reservation in heaven wasn't cheap.

"Listen, Kristy, thanks for checking on me. I'm totally fine. I'm enjoying the solitude before the baby comes. I'm kinda tired, so I think I'm gonna take a nap. I'll text you later, okay?"

"Oh, sure. Yeah, pregnancy is exhausting. Good

idea. Okay." She hung up, leaving me to my limited freedom. The problem with allowing other people to care about you is knowing you are now responsible for keeping in touch with them. This was a chore I did not cherish.

Besides Kristy, the only other people I maintained regular contact with were Angel and Aubrey. Of course, even if I had wanted to get rid of Angel, I couldn't. She had proven her worth to me over and over again throughout my childhood. Even when I was embarrassingly horrid to her, she never gave up. She had a huge heart, filled with dozens of foster kids like me. Although she worked in foster care for her entire career, she wasn't hardened by the emotional toll it must have taken.

I'd known Aubrey for just as long. After I moved in with the Calkins, they pulled me out of public school and plunked me down in a tiny Christian school connected to their church. I met Aubrey on my first day there. She befriended me right away, and we'd been close ever since.

Rising from the floor by the bassinet, I stretched, rolling my shoulders, then twisted to stretch my back until I heard a satisfying pop. *How long have I been sitting there?* Sometimes I seemed to lose track of time. It happened more often than I liked to admit. It was almost as if I was in the middle of a waking dream. I'd be halfway through a task, then suddenly, I found myself in a different room, doing something else. I glanced at my watch. *How much time had just passed?* The baby was still asleep, her rosebud lips still repeating phantom suckling movements.

It was growing dark outside. The sky was now gray

and dim. I shivered and walked over to the small wood-burning stove. Grabbing a piece of wood, I pulled the handle to open the door and threw it in. My stomach growled so loudly that it made me chuckle. Opening the fridge, neatly tucked between the counter and the half wall that made up my bathroom, I grabbed the eggs. They had expired weeks ago. Swallowing down the guilt over wasting food, I tossed the carton in the garbage and grabbed a granola bar instead.

Several weeks ago, on my walk to the corner store, a small homemade sign caught my eye. A pre-teen boy sat at the edge of his front yard by a sign stating he had eggs for sale. Gangly legs spread as he bent over his phone. There weren't too many houses out this way, but I had stopped here before to buy *Leminad* from a little girl at her homemade stand. I pulled on my fabric face mask and gloves. Remembering to keep my distance, I stepped closer, cash already settled in my gloved hand.

"Hi." The kid looked up from his device. He pulled the mask that had been sitting loosely beneath his chin, up and over his mouth and nose. His eyes settled on my enormous belly.

"I didn't know you guys sold eggs. Do you raise chickens?" I asked.

He continued to stare at my middle while nodding his head.

"Yeah, my mom just decided we had enough extra eggs to start selling. Do you live out here?"

Nodding back, I handed him three dollars as he passed me a cardboard carton. "If you bring back the carton next time, my mom says you'll get a free egg. We wrote the expiration date on the sticker for you."

"Huh? Oh, thanks. Yeah. Sure, I can do that."

"So, you're due pretty soon, huh?"

Self-consciously I placed a hand on the mountain my belly had become. "Yup, not long now."

"You should meet my mom." He turned his head toward his house. "Are you delivering at the hospital?" *Nosey kid.* The hospital was about forty-five minutes away. "Um…" *This was a strange conversation to be having with a kid.*

"I mean, I only ask cuz my mom does that kind of stuff."

"Oh." I started. Of course, I hadn't yet quite planned out what to do when I went into labor. Before moving out here, I was keeping up with my appointments. Since the Pandemic started, I had been meeting regularly with my OB online. She wanted me to stay away from the hospital as long as possible, but my plan had been to call for a rideshare when my labor began. *Is this kid for real?* I'd never been the kind of sentimental person who felt that life was full of *signs* or, as Mrs. C would have called it, "Divine Intervention." But this gave me pause. *How perfect could this be? A home delivery!* I had briefly considered it at the beginning of my pregnancy, but my OB didn't do home births, and I just figured a hospital would be the cleanest way to go about the whole thing anyway. I'd also been lazy about reaching out to anyone locally, despite all of the reseach that Kristy had bombarded me with. Quarantine has encouraged my introvertsion and increased my overall anxiety. Perhaps it was *providential* that I met this kid and his mom just happened to deliver babies.

"If you wanna wait here for a minute, I can ask her to come outside and meet you." Tucking his phone into his back pocket, he turned and ran to the house before I could respond.

Chapter Four

August 21, 2020

I pulled my steaming oatmeal from the microwave and sat next to the bassinet. *Do babies have a sixth sense?* As soon as I brought the spoon to my mouth, she started crying. Shoveling the food in, I swore as it burned my tongue. I set the spoon down and picked the baby up.

"Shh. It's okay." I murmured into her wispy blonde hair. "Shh. Are you hungry? Wet? Come on, baby girl, let's check you out. After changing her, I returned her to the bassinet, even though she was still crying. *Am I supposed to keep nursing you? This is so strange.* With mixed emotions and racing thoughts, I lifted her to my breast.

My mind worked overtime as I nursed her. I've always been the type of person who needs a plan. *Do I call the authorities? And, If I do, wouldn't they all come here and see all of my baby stuff? Do I drop her off at a hospital or fire station? If her mother isn't located, she would just go into the foster care system. Do I keep her?* I asked myself the questions I already knew that answer to.

What would be the harm, really? I mean, assuming her mother left her for a good reason. After all, abandoning a baby pretty much means you don't want her. Right? It could be perfect. As long as no one comes back for her, everyone would assume she's mine. I had already begun to claim her.

Looking down at her perfect little face, I traced the outline of her profile. Her nose was so tiny, with the slightest curve extending to the peak. Her eyes, now closed in bliss, were a different shape than my son's. His had the tell-tale almond shape, the extra unmistakable fold. Signs of a life that would be frought with challenges. Her eyes were wide and round, with fine blonde lashes and brows. Lifting her little body up to my shoulder, I burped her and returned her to the bassinet. I had already made up my mind. And, if I was going to keep her, I needed to make some changes.

Standing in the middle of my tiny house, I tried to imagine what this space would look like from an outsider's point of view. Since no one knew the gender of the baby at the time of my baby shower, I had mostly neutral colored items. Grabbing a pastel blue onesie and matching blanket, I looked around for anything else indicative of traditionally male accoutrement that I should remove. The baby's alcove was small. It was basically just a changing table, with two shelves underneath already filled with extra diapers, wipes, onesies, and burp clothes. Usually, the stackable washer and dryer would be in that space, but I hadn't yet saved up enough to purchase them. Since Covid hit, I'd been washing clothes in the kitchen sink and hanging them to dry on the line outside. The cream bassinet was next to the woodburning stove in the living room. I had only hung one baby-related picture on the wall. My baby's sonogram printout was carefully placed in a light green frame. Its legs tucked up, as if purposefully preventing a gender reveal. Most of the walls in my house were a creamy eggshell white, and I liked the look of the sage against the pale wall.

After peeking at the baby one more time, I tiptoed to the door and quietly pulled it open. The sunlight felt good on my skin as I stepped outside. One of the things I liked the most about living out here was the silence. It was a warm night. The sound of cicadas buzzed in the background as I listened for any crying from the baby. No crying.

I made my way back to the rose garden and the small stone I'd had placed over my buried child. Taking a step back from the sacred space, my eyes swept the entirety of my rose garden. Besides the small clearing in the middle of the garden, it was unremarkable. Just in case someone did stop by for a visit, I needed to make sure no one would guess my secret. Following the small path to my vegetable garden, I walked over to the pile of empty pots and planters I had haphazardly shoved to the side. Grabbing two pots and setting the small one inside of the larger one, I used my free hand to lift a small bag of bird seed I'd ordered online a few weeks prior.

I carried the items back to the rose garden. Lifting the small pot out, I turned the large one over and placed it over the rock. Setting the small pot right side up on top of it, I tore into the bag of birdseed and grabbed a few handfuls, tossing them into the small vessel. It wasn't pretty, but it would do for now. Stepping back to survey my makeshift bird feeder, I nodded in satisfaction and returned the open bag of seed to the outdoor closet.

By now, the dusk had followed me inside, so as I

pulled the door shut, I flipped on a few lights. It had been an exhausting day, and although I could feel my body aching for sleep, my stomach was empty. I'd read that nursing a baby meant that you needed extra calories. The thought of even heating up one of the dozen frozen meals I had seemed overwhelming. I carefully pulled the bassinet next to the couch and lay down. My eyes were heavy with fatigue. Before I could think through any other plans, I was fast asleep.

****

The sound of a light tapping on my door woke me. Fear flooded through me as I scrambled up. Amazingly, the baby was still asleep. It was the first time she'd slept through the entire night. I stumbled to the door, peering through the stained-glass window. A colorfully warped version of Angel stood on the other side. Exhaling slowly, I opened the door.

"Did I wake you?" Angel stepped back and adjusted her face mask. Even though we were over seven hours away from the Covid Capital, NYC, the entire state was still under strict quarantine orders. In addition to the protective gear, she was wearing a long sundress. It's sheer fabric hugging her curves.

"It's nearly eight. I got an extra early start today, but I waited in my car till eight, just to be polite." she said.

"It's okay. I needed to get up."

Angel shifted her eyes to my stomach, now considerably smaller than it had been the last time she saw me.

"You had the baby?" Still standing in place, she tried to peer past me. Her brow furrowed in confusion.

"Why didn't you call me? When did you have her?

Is it a girl or a boy? I just saw you, like three weeks ago!"

"Um, yeah, I know." I stalled for time. The first of many lies to trip so easily off of my tongue. "It happened so fast. I was gonna call. I just have been so tired, ya know? It's a girl." Speaking this aloud solidified my decision to claim this child as my own.

"Oh my gosh! Can I see her?" She took a step back. "I mean, I'll stay right here. I won't even breathe in her direction." Angel's eyes wrinkled, and I assumed she was smiling under her mask, giving me her best puppy-dog eyes.

I hesitated for a moment, then turned to get the baby. She opened her eyes as I lifted her gently. Cradling her in my arms, I pulled the door open all the way and stood in its frame.

Angel moved slightly to the side, keeping her distance but straining to get a closer look.

"She's beautiful, Willow. When did you get back from the hospital?"

"A few days ago." I swallowed down the lie. If I told Angel I'd had a home delivery, I knew she'd insist on me going in for a checkup. By making her believe that everything had gone according to plan, she'd assume I was telling her the truth. Lying to Angel had always been so easy.

"What's her name?" Angel adjusted her mask again.

"Zoe." The name popped out before giving it too much thought. Zoe had been on the top of the list of baby names I'd started as a teenager. Saying the name out loud felt good.

"What about her middle name?"

"Elizabeth." I paused, "Zoe Elizabeth Morgan." I rubbed Zoe's back as I took ownership of her.

"So, she's taking your last name?" In the past, Angel had tried to get information about the baby's father from me. As sly as she tried to be, I knew Angel's methods of information gathering.

"Yup. I really should change and feed her." A pungent odor had made its way to my nose.

"Of course. Do you need anything? I can pick up some stuff from the store for you and drop it off." Her generosity always impressed me. I had aged out of the system years ago, yet Angel insisted on remaining a part of my life.

"You are so kind, but I just put an order in this morning." I lied. "I think we are all set."

"Well, maybe the quarantine will be lifted soon, and then I can hold her." She looked longingly at Zoe. "Please call me if you need *anything*. Will you do that, Willow?"

I nodded.

"I mean it. I *know* you're independent and all…but I'm happy to help however I can."

"Thanks, Angel. I know. And, I will."

As she was climbing back into her hybrid, she yelled, "Don't be surprised if I show up again soon with some stuff for you!"

I waved as she did a K-turn out of my small dirt driveway and headed back to the foster kids who still relied on her for a bit of sanity in their dismal lives.

"Zoe," I whispered into the baby's ear. "Welcome home, Zoe. I'm your mom." I pulled the door closed as she nestled her head on my shoulder.

****

To: Melaniewalker@catharsistimepress.com
From: Willowmorgan666@gmail.com
Subject: Age 10

Mel, here's another chapter. Is there anything you want me to change? Stay healthy and safe. -W

"Today is the parade! Today is the parade!" Molly sang the words as she danced around our room. The Calkins had promised to drive us to a nearby suburb so we could watch the festivities. Molly had heard that at some of the local parades, they threw candy to the kids watching.

"Look! This is my bag to catch all the candy! And, I got one for you too, Willow." She presented me with a pillowcase she'd taken from the hall closet. She handed it to me with a curtsy.

"You know we can't use these. Mrs. C would never let us." I held my hand out to take the other case from her. Now I needed to find a way to return them to the closet without Mrs. C seeing me.

"But we need it to be big! I want to have room for all the candy!"

"I know, but don't you have anything else we can use?"

"Let's just ask her if we can use them." Molly took the pillowcases back from me and headed for the door.

"No. Molly, wait." I opened up the toy chest in our room and began to rummage through it.

"Wal-la!" Pulling a large piece of fabric from the bin, I opened it up and wrapped it around my shoulders, dancing around the room. "We can make our own." I spun around in circles as Molly giggled.

Just then, the door opened, and Mrs. C stood there watching us. "What are you doing?"

I stopped mid-spin and met her icy stare. "Nothing." I glanced at Molly, who was still holding the pillowcases.

"Nothing." Molly quickly moved her hands behind her back.

"What's behind your back, Molly?" Mrs. C remained in the doorway.

"Nothing," she repeated.

Mrs. C slowly walked over to Molly. When she was standing right in front of her, she asked again. "I can see you have something behind your back, Molly. Now, be truthful. What is it?"

Molly began to tear up. She shook her head from side to side but remained silent.

"It's not her fault. I borrowed some pillowcases for the parade tonight." I stepped next to Molly and slipped the fabric from her hand. I handed it to Mrs. C. Molly was now studying the floor.

"Look at me, Molly." Mrs. C deepened her voice. Just the change in tone made me look up at her too.

"God knows when you're lying, Molly. So, you might as well just tell me."

Molly looked from me to Mrs. C, and back again. "Um." She began picking at her impossibly short nails.

"Like, I said. It was me. Molly didn't do anything. I—" Mrs. C cut me off.

"Shut up! I'm talking to Molly. We will deal with you later."

"Molly, look at me. It makes Jesus cry when we lie. But you can make Jesus happy by just telling Mommy the truth."

Molly began to cry. She tried to hold it in, but it only resulted in a great sob escaping as a hiccup. "I just,

I just wanted to have a bag for the c-andy." The last word came out as another hiccup.

"So you lied?" Mrs. C's voice continued to rise.

The twins appeared in our bedroom doorway. They were smart enough to remain silent.

"Liars go to hell, Molly. Do you want to go to hell?"

Molly shook her head while tears streamed down her face.

"And you." She turned to me, grabbing my arm. "You lied too! Just wait until your father gets home."

Snatching the pillowcases from my hand, she continued pulling me by the arm across the room and toward the bed.

"Kneel down." She commanded.

I knelt on the space of hard wood between the throw rug and the edge of my bed.

"You too." She began walking toward Molly, who scrambled to her bedside and quickly knelt down before Mrs. C reached her.

"Your father will be home in an hour. I want you both to ask God for forgiveness for your lying tongues. The devil is the father of all lies. Do you want to be a vessel of the devil?"

I had no idea what she was even talking about, but I could see Molly shaking her head, so I copied her.

"Go ahead. Pray to Jesus, right now." We both looked at her for further direction. "I want to hear you ask God for forgiveness for your sins. Lying is a sin. If you want to be cleansed by the blood of Jesus, you need to repent."

This lady was crazy. I had no idea what she was even talking about. No one had ever taught me how to pray. I had seen people pray at the church they dragged us to every Sunday, but no one had ever forced me to my knees to say some kind of magic words by my bed.

We spent our time in Sunday School drinking pineapple juice from huge metal cans and munching on shortbread cookies while they told us happy stories about Jesus and miracles.

"Dear heavenly father," Molly began, repeating the phrase often used by Mr. C at the dinner table each night. "Please forgive me for my sin of lying. Please let me go to heaven when I die." Molly kept her eyes closed and remained by her bedside. I took the opportunity to repeat her magical words.

Mrs. C broke the silence. "Good." she nodded in approval. "Very good. Jesus died on the cross so that he could forgive all of your sins. Willow, go get the big Bible from the living room and bring it back here, please." I stood and slowly made my way toward the door. Molly had opened her eyes, but they remained fixed on the side of her bed. I walked past the twins, down the hallway, following the stairs to the living room. The book took up a third of the coffee table. It was hardcover, etched in gold with matching gilded edges. I lifted it awkwardly, wrapping both arms around it as it thumped against my belly. It took me longer to make it back up the stairs without dropping it. When I finally returned to the room, the twins were gone, and Molly was sitting on the bed.

"Girls, I am disappointed in you both. You should have just asked me for bags in the first place. You certainly shouldn't have lied to me when I asked you about what you were holding. You will both get spanked when your father gets home. The Bible teaches us we must train up our children in the way of the Lord. Just this week, Pastor Mettin told us of the importance of not sparing the rod and spoiling the child. Now, girls, I want you to find a Bible verse that teaches us about obeying our parents. Take your time, and find a verse about obedience. Then I want you each to write that verse one hundred times."

Molly began to cry again. Although she had just finished the first grade, she hated writing. Many of her letters were still written backward, and sometimes the letters were so large, she often finished by flipping the page over to write on the other side.

"You can use the paper and pencils in your desk. Go ahead and get started. I have to get dinner ready." She sauntered away, taking the frigid air with her.

I waited until I heard her go all the way down the stairs before tiptoeing to the door and closing it softly.

"I'm sorry." Molly began to cry again.

"Shh." I went over and sat next to her on the flowered bedspread. "You didn't do anything wrong. This is so stupid," I muttered.

"But we lied. And Jesus doesn't let liars into heaven. I don't want to go to hell, Willow."

"Shh. I don't even know what she is talking about." I rubbed small circles on Molly's back. "Do you really think we would go to hell for taking pillowcases out of the closet?"

Molly shrugged her shoulders and gave me a sad smile.

"Come on, let's get this over with." I cracked open the large book, and we began flipping through the pages.

Chapter Five

August 28, 2020

I once read that the first seven years of life are the most important. Those formative years are the ones setting the groundwork for our future selves So the way I figure, if I could manage to keep this baby unscathed for seven more years, she'd have a fighting chance in this world. After all, I did my homework. I read countless baby and parenting books throughout my pregnancy. And, if there was indeed a God, maybe I had been given a chance to create the childhood I never had.

For the past week, I had been tiptoeing around my own house with bated breath. Every hour that passed by without someone forcing their way into my home and taking Zoe away from me was a step closer to creating my new reality. This morning I woke up happy. I lay in bed for a brief, blissful moment. Joy was an emotion I didn't often succumb to. That's the thing about happiness; it never lasts long and is usually followed by suffering. Pushing the dark thoughts aside, I eased my way to the edge of the bed to peer over the side at Zoe. My bedroom ceiling was low. Sitting up in bed only allotted a few inches between the top of my head and the skylight.

Back when I started looking at tiny houses, I

searched for something that would have extra floor space along one side of the bed. My queen-sized bed took up nearly the entire loft, leaving about two feet of open floor space between the steps and the mattress. It gave me a little bit of space to make the bed in the morning, and on the days I remembered to bring a change of clothes with me to the loft, it was perfect for standing and getting dressed. The bassinet fit snugly along the wall, and Zoe continued to slumber. Like clockwork, she woke me every three hours throughout the night. To my surprise, her demand for milk increased my supply. I was beginning to have moments where I looked at her and forgot she wasn't mine. *Would I eventually see her as my very own child? Would I ever forget for a moment about the loss of my son?*

As Zoe continued to sleep, I pulled my robe off the hook on the wall and wrapped myself in its warmth. Climbing down the stairs, I shuffled into the kitchen to make some coffee. I stood looking at my neatly lined up jars of coffee, flour, sugar, and spices. Angel had been hinting for years that I had some obsessive-compulsive traits. I smiled as I recalled the time she took me to a psychiatrist.

****

To: Melaniewalker@catharsistimepress.com
From:Willowmorgan666@gmail.com
Subject: Age 15
Mel, did I ever tell you about the time I saw my psychiatrist ahead of me at the drive-thru? It was surreal. I imagine he was ordering the greasiest, most unhealthy food on the menu and then shoveling it into his mouth as he drove away. It made me like him even

more. -W

At fifteen, I was miserable in my own skin, and I'd begun picking at my face. At first, it wasn't a big deal. I'd notice a bump or blemish and begin picking at it, trying to make my skin even and smooth. Eventually, I started picking at things that weren't even really there. My face was pinpricked with angry red marks left from hours of mindless picking.

Angel insisted on taking me to a psychiatrist. He was a caricature of a man. In fact, it took all of my teenage willpower to not laugh when he first came into the room. I thought perhaps he was playing a joke of some kind on me. Was there a hidden camera gauging my reaction to him? He was extremely tall, over six feet, and had pitch black hair. The kind of blackness that can only be achieved with chemicals.

He wore a three-piece royal blue suit. I had never had a good sense of gaydar, but his outfit seemed to suggest he may prefer the company of other men. The tipping point was his bowtie. It was pink with tiny blue stars on it. His shiny, black dress shoes matched both his hair and his horn-rimmed glasses.

Despite my years in foster care, I had never met a psychiatrist before. I'd managed to stay under the radar by complying with almost any and all requests adults made of me. Until the skin-picking, no one had managed to pick up on the fact that I was brimming with anxiety.

"Miss Morgan," he began as he motioned for me to sit in the oversized leather chair, "Why don't we start with discussing what brings you here today?"

I studied his earnest face. He seemed nice enough. For some reason, I had the deluded thought that he could read my mind. Perhaps by simply looking at me, he could see the darkness I had inside. I squirmed under his kind gaze.

"Well, I guess I'm here because my caseworker made me come." I crossed my arms and waited for him to respond. When he only silently smiled at me, I sighed and continued.

"I kinda pick at my skin," I mumbled.

He waited to see if I would continue. When I didn't, he leaned forward in his chair without breaking eye contact. The intensity of his gaze was a bit overwhelming to me. Up until now, I had perfected the art of invisibility. Compliance and obedience were rewarded at the Calkins'. Anything less than that was deemed to be ungodly, and some sort of strange punishment would be doled out.

"Why do you think that is?" he inquired.

"What?" I shifted my gaze to the floor.

"Why do you think you pick at your skin?" No one had asked me this simple question. I had been reprimanded for it, punished, and made fun of. No one had ever bothered to ask me why. I had no idea why I did it. I just did it.

"I dunno. I guess I'm just messed up."

"Why do you say that?"

I paused, trying to choose my words carefully. "I guess because most other people don't pick at their face till it bleeds?"

"Hmm. Maybe not. But I suspect everyone has some type of habit they'd like to change. Is this something you'd like to change?"

Looking around the room, it was apparent that this guy was both highly educated and that he had a lot of patients. There was a stack of manilla folders by his chair. It was so high it had begun to slide, tipping over just enough for a few documents to have spilled onto the floor. His wall was covered with diplomas, awards, and certificates. Yet, he talked to me like a regular person. He didn't seem mad at me, disappointed, or even that fake type of friendliness that drove me crazy.

"I guess." I looked back into his bespectacled blue eyes. Through the thick lenses, they appeared huge. When he remained silent, I continued.

"I mean, I think other people want me to stop. So, I guess so."

"Why do you think that other people want you to stop?"

Rolling my eyes, I gave a quick laugh. "Probably cuz they don't want to keep looking at my face anymore? Probably because I keep missing the bus because I spent too much time in front of the mirror? Probably because they are embarrassed by me?" Besides Angel, this was the longest conversation I'd had with an adult in years. Since I was a quiet, compliant kid, no one usually bothered to pay me too much attention.

"I find it interesting you mention how your skin picking affects others. For example, you talk about others having to look at you or being embarrassed by you. But I wonder how you feel about the picking?"

"I guess I don't think much about it. I mean, when I pass by a mirror, I stop. And if I see any kind of bump or scab, I just start picking at it."

"Do you know about how much time you spend each day picking?" His tone was kind, inquisitive, yet not intrusive.

"I dunno. I've never timed it." My words dripped with acid. When I met his eyes, I felt as though he could see past the marks on my face. It didn't scare him off. He waited to see if I was going to continue talking, and when I didn't, he quietly responded.

"Willow, I understand from Angel that you've had a bit of a rough life so far. Since you signed a release form, she told me a little bit about the foster homes you've been in. It sounds like you've been moved around a bit, and you've been with the Calkin family for the last five years now, right?"

I nodded. I could feel the pinprick of tears threatening to expose my weakness.

"How are things with the Calkins?"

I shrugged and swallowed the lump in my throat but remained silent. After what felt like an eternity, he spoke quietly.

"I grew up in foster care, too."

This caused me to look up and stop the picking at my nails that I hadn't even realized I'd started.

"It sucked. And it made it really hard for me to trust other people, especially adults."

I held my breath as he continued.

"So it took me a while to feel safe enough to open up to other people and talk about all the stuff going on in my head."

He gave me a small smile and leaned forward in his chair. "What would you think of coming back to talk to me again sometime soon?"

"Are we done?" I wanted to hear more about his time in foster care. How had he become so successful? Maybe I was too messed up for him to help me? My thoughts swirled like the kaleidoscope of colors in the painting above his desk. He stood and made his way toward the door.

"I wish we had more time to talk, but I'm afraid that's all the time we have today." He pushed his glasses up further on his nose.

"Aren't you gonna prescribe me some pills or something?"

"Do you feel like you need pills for something?"

"Do you always answer a question with another question?"

A tiny laugh escaped despite his attempt at keeping a straight face. "Sometimes. But mostly, I just like to listen. And I think you have a lot to say. So, would you consider coming back to talk soon?" I felt a tiny bit of disappointment creeping up my spine but I nodded. "In the meantime," he continued, "I'm wondering if you would consider doing one thing for me? A type of homework, if you will."

"Homework?" I rolled my eyes again as he laughed.

"I promise it's not hard."

"Okay."

"Okay, I'd like to recommend you start writing in a journal every day."

"Like a prayer journal?" Mrs. Calkins had given each of us prayer journals for Easter. She insisted we write down our prayers to God every day, along with our thoughts about the Bible chapters they assigned us to read daily. I hated it. I rolled my eyes and sighed loudly.

"More like a journal that is just for you. Write about whatever you like—how you are feeling, things that annoy you, whatever you want." He handed me a small diary. It was covered in pink and white hearts and had a small silver lock and key attached. "I know this one is really meant for a younger child, but I thought perhaps you would appreciate the lock. Plus, it's small enough that you can hide it easily."

I nodded as he handed it to me.

"How about we meet again in two weeks?"

I nodded again, trying to hold in my smile. I'd never been good at emotional stuff, but I somehow felt a little bit lighter already. He held out his hand, and I timidly shook it.

"It was a pleasure to talk to you today, Willow. I look forward to next time." I followed him out to the waiting room, where Mrs. C sat reading a magazine. The journal already tucked into my denim purse.

Chapter Six

September 20, 2020

Social distancing was now the norm. Since I was fairly self-sufficient and ordered most of my stuff online, I hadn't needed to venture out much since the pandemic began. But from the look of things on the news, life wasn't changing anytime soon. In fact, gatherings of any kind were prohibited once again. Not wearing a mask in public would result in immediate ostracization, not to mention the potential risk of killing someone by inadvertently carrying an invisible virus.

Yesterday my uncle sent me a message, asking if he could stop by. We were certainly not comfortable enough with each other for him to randomly visit without advance notice. He had sent me a message recently, asking if the baby had been born. I eventually replied by sending him a photo of Zoe. This morning he messaged again, saying that he wanted to stop by to drop off a small gift and meet Zoe. He assured me he would stay outside and wear his face mask.

It was nearly three p.m. by the time I heard a small rapping at my door. Zoe was asleep, so I scooped her up and made my way over to the entrance. My front door was another feature of my tiny house I adored.

Angel and I took a trip to a county building that the city was planning to demolish. She had a friend who was on the demo team, and he brought us to the site a few days before the demolition was scheduled.

The old brick building used to house psychiatric patients until the state closed it down in 1983. It had been sitting in disrepair ever since. As soon as I saw the abandoned door, I knew I had to have it. The hinges had already been removed, and it was leaning against a dilapidated wall. Despite the crumbling, moldy building, the door was in good condition. The dark wood was etched with intricate winding vines and flowers. Its design was both comforting and charming.

The best part, however, was the fact that it was a Dutch door. The top half of the door is linked to the bottom by a simple iron latch. The latch itself was rusted and broken, but could easily be fixed. Within the upper half of the door was a small but beautiful circular stained-glass window. Amazingly, the glass was still intact. Green ivy surrounded the circle of glass. Inside of the ivy was a beautiful white lily.

Finding that door brought me such satisfaction. Angel was able to sweet-talk the contractor and a friend of his to carry it out of the building, wrap it and load it into his truck. For twenty dollars, he later drove out to my property. And, after a bit of measurement adjustments, it was mine.

Opening the top portion of the door, I hesitantly stood with Zoe snuggling against me. My uncle took a step back and set a gift bag on the front step. His surgical mask was pulled tight around his nose and mouth, causing his wire-rim glasses to fog up. He tilted his face to peer underneath them at us.

"She's beautiful, Willow." I smiled at him from the interior of my house. Technically, I should probably be wearing a mask, but I figured the space between us left room for the air to blow away any potential Covid germs.

"Thank you." Over the years, we had barely interacted. Our conversations always felt courteous but awkward. Today wasn't any different.

"I'm sorry I didn't come by earlier. I thought maybe you would be too nervous with the pandemic and all to have any visitors."

I nodded. "I think if you just stay there, we should be all right." I turned Zoe around so she was facing outward.

"I brought you a few things." He pointed to the small gift bag by his feet. "Your Aunt wiped them all down. But you can disinfect them again, of course."

"Thank you." Zoe began to wiggle against me. She was getting hungry and would probably start crying soon. I shifted her position.

"She looks like Susan."

"Really?" Susan was his youngest daughter. The prettiest. I followed her online and knew she had moved to California. The tanned faces of her own children plastered her page.

"That's cool." *I sound so lame.* I hated small talk.

"Well," he cleared his throat. "I brought some extra wood for your stove, so I'll just stack it out back for you."

"What do I owe you?" *What if he notices the loose dirt by the rosebushes? Will he suspect anything?*

"Don't worry about it. Everything else working okay? Need anything?"

"I think we are okay." *Would I ever feel comfortable around him? Was he just being nice to make up for lost time? Did it really even matter?*

"Okay, well, I'll just leave this here." He gestured to the gift bag by his feet. "I'm going to head home, but let me know if you need anything. I can always stop by."

He shifted his weight, and I wondered if he felt as uncomfortable as I did.

"She's beautiful, Willow. Congratulations. I mean it. Please let me know if you need anything. I can be here at a moment's notice. It's only a mile."

I nodded. *It might as well be one hundred miles.*

"I'd better go. Your aunt gets really nervous these days if I'm gone too long."

"Okay. Thanks again." He smiled at us and waved before turning to head back to his truck for the wood.

****

To: Melaniewalker@catharsistimepress.com
From:Willowmorgan666@gmail.com
Subject: Age 10

Mel, Here's what I came up with for the newest chapter. Thanks again for the suggestions for the last section. I'll work on getting the revisions back to you by the end of the week. -W.

School was not a place of respite for me. Kids are cruel, especially girls. But, when you're a foster kid, it's as if you are walking around with a scarlet letter on or something. Until moving in with the Calkins, I'd only known public school. Even though the school year was half over, I was pulled out of my fourth-grade class and plunked into a rinky-dink Christian school. I'm not exaggerating when I say that it was small. In fact, the fourth-grade class was so small, they combined it with the fifth grade. Between the two classes, which were taught by one teacher in a large room, there were sixteen of us. Since I was a quiet kid, I never got into trouble. However, being quiet didn't serve me well as far as trying to fit in with my peers. When you are in a class of sixteen, there isn't much blending in going on.

The school was housed in the basement of a large church. Faithful Followers Congregation had built the church back in the seventies. By 1980, the congregation had grown so much that they built classrooms in the basement and added a large gymnasium. To enter the school, you had to go through a set of double glass doors, walk past the sanctuary, and down another flight of stairs. The gray-green carpet was well-worn and seemed to emit the smell of feet despite all the frequent rug shampooing the custodian did.

Once during our prayer circle, the girl kneeling alongside me actually started dry heaving after they asked us to switch from sitting at our desks to kneeling on the floor beside our chairs for our daily prayer. After the teacher sent her to the bathroom, he allowed us to move back into our chairs. From then on, that's where we remained for morning prayer. The school was basically a long narrow hallway, with sparsely filled classrooms on either side. At the end of the hallway stood the principal's office, along with a tiny room for his secretary. My classroom was large, with fourth graders on one side of the room and fifth graders on the other. The desks were the small metal type, with smooth wooden tops that flipped up to open. Principal Pearce walked me down the smelly hallway and opened the door to my new classroom. As soon as he did, the room fell silent as fifteen heads turned toward me. I followed my shoes to the only open desk, which happened to be in the front row.

"Class, this is Willowmina Morgan. She is staying with the Calkin family."

"Willow," I whispered as I slumped into the metal chair.

"Pardon?" Mr. Pearce squatted down beside me. Despite his friendly tone, he sounded annoyed with me.

"Please call me Willow." I said quietly.

"Ahh, yes, Willow." He stood to proclaim it to the rest of the class. "And you shall take on the first day the fruit of the splendid trees, branches of palm trees and bows of leafy trees and willows of the brook, and you shall rejoice before the Lord your God seven days. Leviticus 23:40." He smiled down at me as I pretended to know what he was talking about.

The teacher stepped away from his desk and took a small step in my direction. I let out my breath silently as the principal exited.

"Welcome, Willow. I'm Mr. Maddenowski, but everyone just calls me Mr. M." A few of the girls giggled.

"Let's all welcome Willow, shall we?"

I could feel the heat creeping up my chest into my cheeks as they all welcomed me in a sing-song chorus of sorts.

"It's not easy to start at a new school halfway through the year." He gave me a slight nod. "Welcome." Turning, he moved over to the chalkboard.

The rest of my first day was a blur. I tried to keep my head down and draw as little attention to myself as possible. The hand-me-down clothes didn't help, though. I kept tugging at the sleeves of my Oxford, wishing it covered my wrists. The stiff white material was itchy, hot, and ugly. I couldn't wait to get home and change.

"I hate these stupid uniforms." An unusually tall girl with beautiful red curls sat down next to me at lunch. I watched her unwrap her sandwich and rip off a corner before popping it in her mouth.

"Yeah, they kinda suck," I said, noticing as her eyebrows lifted slightly at the word *suck* as she offered me her tiny bag of chips.

"Want these?" She offered the brand name prize to me as if it was no big deal.

"Oh, thanks, but I don't want to take them from you." I loved chips and had only had the brand name ones a few times before.

"Seriously," She pushed them across the table to me. "I ate like three bags of them after school yesterday. I'm kinda tired of them."

"Um, okay then. Thanks." I tried to look graceful as I shoved one into my already-watering mouth.

"I'm Aubrey." She ripped off another piece of sandwich. I had never seen anyone eat so delicately.

"Willow."

"I know. The whole Bible verse thing..." She laughed. "He is always looking for a reason to quote the Bible. It drives me crazy."

Remaining silent, I gorged myself on the salty goodness.

Aubrey continued to talk to me as if we were old friends. "So, you live with the Calkins, huh?" I nodded, crunching noisily.

"Sorry to hear that. I probably shouldn't say anything, but that must..." She paused and looked around before whispering, "suck."

This time I laughed. It looked like maybe I actually was making a friend.

****

Faithful Followers was known for its evangelical services. Not only did I spend my school week there, but the Friday night and Sunday morning and evening services were mandatory in the Calkins house. Church became my whole world. No outside friends were allowed. The radio, or any other type of secular music, was forbidden. Even library books I checked out weekly had to be approved by my foster parents. Books containing magic, rebellious kids, or any hint of sexuality were prohibited.

Once, a book I'd borrowed had a drawing of a girl in a yoga pose on the cover. Mrs. Calkins confiscated it until she could return it to the library. Apparently, yoga was somehow connected to the occult. After being forced to listen to a half-hour lecture about the dark arts and energies, I felt defeated. Even the excitement of escaping through books was being taken from me.

In retrospect, my life in foster care could have been much worse. At the time, I felt both lonely and isolated. Each year I spent in the protective environment of the church, I became more and more terrified of inadvertently sinning, and damning myself to an eternity in a fiery pit of misery.

Chapter Seven

April 11, 2021

Maybe motherhood is meant to keep you so busy that you don't have time to feel lonely. I'd always struggled with anxiety. Perhaps that's part of what makes me feel so separate from others.

The first few months of quarantine were a welcome respite of sorts, an easy excuse to drop out of society without the added pressure of an explanation. My connection to the world had always felt disjointed. It was as if I moved through life with a bubble of protection around me.

A film of tragic ectoplasm coated my existence. The trauma of past generations clung to me, and constant internal chatter kept me company. Every thought was plagued by my desire to be liked even as I kept the word at a distance. Each word I did choose to speak was carefully chosen and then dissected for flaws and self-judgment. Long before Covid, I was acutely aware as each surface I touched left me covered with microscopic germs I could never successfully wash away. Everyone else was finally living with the type of tangible anxiety I'd long been accustomed to.

I patted Zoe on the back, urging a burp while I thought back to the first night I spent in foster care...

I was trying to fall asleep on the small cot in a

stranger's living room. I lay in the dimly lit room, while the glow of the television flickered on my face. Closing my eyes, I began rapidly turning my head back and forth, back and forth, rubbing my hair into the pillow as I tried to lull myself to sleep. Suddenly, a light hand touched my arm. I gasped, opening my eyes to see a lovely, dark face peering down at me.

"Chiquita, why is it you do this?" She copied my exaggerated movement. Her head swaggered from side to side at an alarming speed.

"Huh?" Sitting up, I shrugged silently. The head movement had become part of my bedtime routine. I had been doing it as long as I could remember. It was the only way I could get to sleep.

I began crying, embarrassed, and unsure of what to do with myself.

"Shh, shhh chiquita, is okay. You do what you do. Shh, is okay." She smoothed my bangs off of my forehead and continued to do so until I settled back down and pretended to fall asleep. After she left the room, I started rocking my head back and forth again, lulled into a false sense of comfort. If only I could have stayed with this kind stranger longer. Apparently her home was only used before more permanent foster homes were located.

Zoe burped loudly, pulling me away from my murky thoughts. I propped her up against me as I stood and walked into the kitchen. Although I could video chat with Aubrey or Angel, somehow doing so left me feeling lonelier. Jellybeans and donuts had become my loyal friends. I had begun turning to them for solace on a daily basis. My stomach and ass had been suffering as a result, and I was now almost back to the weight I was while pregnant. *What does it matter anyway? It's not like I have anybody to impress.* Zoe watched me as I opened my pantry and scooped my hand into the small glass bowl of candy.

"Don't judge me," I muttered as I shoved a few into my mouth.

Each day with Zoe was a joy. I began to realize I'd been living my entire life with bated breath, always waiting for something "bad" to happen. Somehow, the love I felt for her was changing me. I woke each morning exhausted but with purpose. My part-time job as a freelance writer paid the few bills I had, but it never exactly made me feel fulfilled.

Despite all the warnings from the baby books I'd been reading, Zoe sometimes slept in bed with me. I rolled up a bath towel and put it between her and the space between the mattress and the wall. Since I was terrified that I would roll over on her in my sleep, I filled one of my knee socks with tennis balls and tucked the lumpy tube along my side each night. The few times I'd rolled in her direction, I'd awakened immediately. Thankfully, my strange child-proofing had worked perfectly!

When I woke this morning, I was alarmed to see Zoe had turned onto her stomach in her sleep. She had rolled over for the first time earlier in the week. I was bummed that I didn't catch it with my camera phone but glad I'd witnessed it. Not that I ever really let her out of my sight. Even when I had to use the bathroom or shower, I placed her in the bouncy seat that I'd gotten as a gift. Since the bathroom was so small, Zoe would bounce slightly from the doorway. Soon she would outgrow the seat, and once she started to crawl, having her in the bed with me was probably not the best idea.

I was just about to shovel another handful of jelly beans into my mouth when my phone rang. Not many people actually *talked* on the phone anymore, so a slight feeling of dread worked its way across my chest at the thought of conversing out loud. It was Aubrey. Although we had video chatted a few times since Zoe's arrival, I couldn't think of the last time Aubrey had actually, old-fashioned called me. Swiping the green icon, I accepted the call and turned it on speakerphone mode.

"Hi. Are you okay?" I breathed a sigh of relief after hearing the joy in her reply.

"What? I'm good. No, I'm *great!*" She laughed.

"Well, that's good. What's going on?"

"Brian proposed!" she yelled. Zoe started to whimper, so I lowered the volume.

"Oh wow. That's great! How did he do it?" I caught myself rolling my eyes and silently chastised myself. If she was happy, I should be happy too.

"Well, you know Brian." She laughed. "He isn't really the *romantic* type."

I thought back to the story she told me about last year's Valentine's Day. Her birthday falls on the same day, and I thought he had made some progress when he presented her with flowers. Until of course, she found the tiny card that had slipped between the lilies that read, *In Sympathy.* It turns out Brian pulled his car over at a funeral home after seeing the bouquet by the garbage can and had rescued them for her. Although I found the gesture distasteful, she still defended his effort at romance.

"It was actually during a commercial. We were watching the news, and a story had just come on about a couple who had been married for sixty-two years. They lived together in a nursing home. It was actually pretty sweet."

"Hold up." I shifted Zoe onto my hip and set the phone on the couch. "He proposed to you during a *commercial*? *Really?"*

She laughed. "I know how ridiculous it sounds. But it was actually really sweet. He muted the TV and turned to me, and said, "I want that to be us. In sixty-two years. Let's do it. Let's get married!"

My mind raced as I remained silent.

"Are you there?"

"Yes, sorry. I mean, was there a *ring?"*

"Yeah, of course. I mean, he ran out of the room and up the stairs. When he came back down, he had this little black box with him. He got down on his knee and everything."

Aubrey and Brian had been living together for the past two years. They started dating almost a year prior. They had talked about getting married, but I had secretly hoped he would get hit by a bus or something. The joy in her voice was palpable. I couldn't ruin her "special moment."

"Congratulations, Aub. Really. I'm happy for you."

"Are you?" she sighed into the phone.

"Of course I am. I guess I was just hoping for a bigger gesture for you. Ya know? Not during a *commercial break."*

"It isn't the *gesture* that matters as much as the relationship, Willow." She huffed, then remained silent until I spoke again. Seeing as I'd never had a relationship lasting for more than a few months, I couldn't exactly debate her point.

"Congratulations, Aubrey. You know I just want the best for you." Zoe sneezed.

"Aww, ZoZo." She broke the slight tension between us. "I bet she is getting so big!"

"She is. I wish you could see her. In person, I mean. It's kinda sad. She's gonna think that social distancing is normal. Like, this is how it's always been for her. She's gonna think people have masks for mouths."

"I know. I wish we lived closer."

Aubrey had moved to Pennsylvania after Brian had a job offer there last year. Granted, it was only a three-hour drive, but I hadn't ventured out there even prior to the Pandemic hitting. Now it felt like I'd never get to see Aubrey's or her new house. The sting of her absence felt like a hot stone in my chest.

"Why don't you come out here? Stay for a few weeks."

"Yeah, right. In the middle of a *pandemic*?" I felt another pang of loneliness in my chest.

"I mean it. Both Brian and I have been working from home since March. We have been super careful. So far, we've managed to stay healthy. It should be safe. You and Zoe can stay with us. We even put a full-sized tub with jets in the new bathroom downstairs. It would be so fun!" I could hear the excitement building in Aubrey's voice as she began to babble.

"*Please,* Willow. I feel like I'm going crazy being pent up for so long. It would be *amazing* to see you and to meet Zoe in person!"

Crouching down to the floor, I propped Zoe up on

her belly, using the baby support pillow. She hates tummy time, but I'd read that it was good for her. I sprinkled some toys around her on the fleece blanket and lay down next to her while she stared at me. Her scrunched-up, angry face made me laugh.

"What's so funny?" Aubrey sighed into the phone.

"Oh, sorry. Zoe is just making her angry face. It's super cute." Aubrey was silent. I knew she was waiting for my answer. "I don't know, Aub. What about my house? The plants and everything?"

"The *plants*? Really? Come on, Willow. Can't you ask your uncle to come water them? Isn't Zoe getting big enough to travel? You could still work online from here, right? Hell, bring the plants with you!"

I watched Zoe's face as she gummed the cushion beneath her. A large spot of drool darkened the fabric. She must be teething. At least she wasn't crying like she normally did when I put her on her stomach. I was stalling for time. Of course, seeing Aubrey would be amazing. It was Brian that I didn't want to have to hang out with. He had always been cordial to me, but if I was being completely honest with myself, I was jealous. He had stolen my best friend from me. Occasionally video chatting just wasn't the same. We used to do everything together. Even something as mundane as grocery shopping could be transformed into an exciting girl's day out with Aubrey.

A text popped up on my phone while she was speaking. I allowed myself a quick peek.

My mom wanted me to tell you she got a free case of formula sent to the house. Do you need anything? Formula? A hot guy to drop by? Anything?

"Willow? Are you even listening to me?"

"Yeah, no. I mean, I am." I flipped the phone over, hoping the speaker wouldn't pick up the noise. Maybe this was just what I needed. To get away. Even further away. I mean, really, what was holding me here? It's not like I saw much of anyone anyway. Work was mobile, so why not?

"Okay." Zoe had begun to whimper, so I turned her around so she was propped into a sitting position. She was getting stronger, and could almost sit on her own.

"Really? Oh my gosh, this is gonna be awesome!" she shouted.

I laughed at her excitement as my own joy bubbled into my throat. "Are you *sure* Brian won't mind?"

"Nah. He won't mind at all. We've got plenty of room! I'm doing a happy dance right now! When can you come?"

"Um, I dunno. I mean, do you want to talk to Brian about it first and call me back or something?"

"Are you kidding? And, run the risk of having you change your mind? He's cool. I promise! Besides, we've talked about it before, and he was all for it! When can you come? Tomorrow?"

I laughed again as I stood and walked over to the kitchen cupboard. Keeping one eye on Zoe, I shoved my hand into the candy jar.

"Tomorrow? Um, that's kind of soon…" She cut me off.

"What else do you have going on? Come tomorrow, before you change your mind."

She knew me too well. I ran through a list of things Zoe and I would need. Packing up my car wouldn't take long at all.

"Okay. Tomorrow."

"Yay!"

"But *only* if you triple-check with Brian and call me right back if he seems hesitant at all."

"Okay, Okay." She laughed.

"Promise?"

"I promise. Now, go start packing. I'm gonna put an order of groceries in. Text me if you think of anything you might need. Oh my gosh, I'm so excited! And text me before you leave tomorrow, okay?"

"Okay."

"You're not gonna change your mind, are you?"

Even though I loved spending time with her, I'd canceled plans at the last minute with her many times over the years. Sometimes the allure of making plans, and then canceling them was just so satisfying. But it seemed safe enough. If they were continuing to social distance, and I clearly was, what was the harm?

"No. I'll come. *We'll* come."

I held the phone away from my ear as she squealed. Zoe turned toward the noise.

"I'm gonna go start packing. I'll text you in the morning."

"Okay. Don't cancel, okay? Please come."

"I'll come. Talk to you tomorrow." I clicked off the phone in the middle of another squeal noting the heat of excitement creep into my chest.

Chapter Eight

To: Melaniewalker@catharsistimepress.com
From:Willowmorgan666@gmail.com
Subject: Age 11

Mel, this one was rough. I actually spent all of my last therapy session talking about it. Do you think readers will find it interesting, or is this all just some kind of rage-writing exercise only for me? Are you in cahoots with my therapist? JK. Let me know what you think. -W

Pastor Mettin screamed at us from the pulpit. "Without Jesus in your heart, you will be damned to an eternity of hell, fire, and brimstone!"

Dragging the softly padded chair underneath the ceiling speaker, I turned the knob until the room became silent. I hated church. In addition to the services lasting two hours or more, most of the sermons were screamed at us. We were constantly reminded of our sinful nature. God was a jealous, demanding entity. Always testing our faith through trials and tribulations. From what I could see, I was a mistake away from damnation.

My one saving grace was working in the nursery. When I first moved in with the Calkins, I would walk by the thick wooden Dutch door and peek in at the babies. Soon, it became a weekly ritual. Armed with my Bible in its snug floral case, I would stand outside the half-door, peering over its smooth wood. Finally, a few weeks after I started doing this, a kind woman with dark hair invited me in.

"Would you like to come in and visit?" Her gentle voice was soothing and inviting. Long, black tresses were wrapped up loosely, forming a thick bun at the base of her head. I had seen her hair down once and was amazed at its length. It reached all the way down to her butt. Perhaps she wore it up to keep it from tumbling into the toilet when she used it?

I nodded in silence, and she opened the door for me to enter.

The nursery was a stark contrast to the rest of the church. Its plush blue carpet greeted me as I looked down at her feet and noticed they were bare. Silently, I slipped off my flats, lining them up alongside hers at the edge of the room. There were only three children here today. One was asleep in one of the many cribs built into the walls. Another child, nestled on her hip. The third, a toddler, sat on the floor. She looked up expectantly and then offered me her drool-covered toy.

"It's okay. You can sit down and play with her. That's Marcia, my daughter. This one," she patted the baby in her arms, "is also mine. His name is Ezekiel. I'm Mrs. Stevens. But you can just call me Mrs. S."

I nodded.

"You're Willow, right?" I raised my eyebrows, surprised she knew my name.

"It's a big place, but we all kind of know each other." She laughed lightly. The sound reminded me of bells at Christmas time.

"You live with the Calkins', right?"

I nodded again, sinking down next to Marcia as she

continued to gnaw on the wooden block.

"You're a quiet one." She smiled and sank down onto the carpet beside me.

Clearing my throat, I responded. "Thank you for letting me come in." I looked around the room, my gaze lingering on the wall of cribs. I had never seen anything like it. The entire wall was made up of cribs. They were nailed to the wall itself. Three rows of connected cribs, with five cribs in each row. The protective wooden bars were pulled down on each one, even though most were empty. I imagined that is what they would use in an orphanage. Last week in school we learned about the sad orphanages in Korea. My eyes pricked with the memory of the photos in our social studies textbooks.

"It's so quiet here," I whispered.

She nodded, then looked up at the circular speaker in the ceiling. "Don't tell, but I turned it off for a bit."

Marcia placed a damp hand on my arm and began pulling herself up to stand beside me.

"We are supposed to listen to the sermon when we are in here, but sometimes it's just nice to enjoy the quiet."

Suddenly, Marcia threw her chubby arms around me, giving me a sticky hug.

Mrs. S laughed. "She loves her hugs. Is she bothering you? Do you want me to move her?"

I shook my head as I held my breath while she continued to hold on.

"Marcia, maybe Willow would read you a book?"

The child plopped herself into my lap and snuggled against me. The warmth of her small body against my chest felt like what I imagined love felt like.

Mrs. S stood, swinging the baby onto her other hip

as she walked over to a basket of books in the corner. "She loves this one. Would you mind reading to her while I change his diaper?"

I took the book from her outstretched hand and opened its thick cardboard pages. Marcia set her tiny hand on my arm while I read. I marveled at her miniscule fingernails, feeling a happy warmth settle in my stomach.

****

April 12, 2021

Packing was harder than I thought it would be. For such a small person, Zoe already had a lot of stuff. In addition to our clothes, I put a box of diapers and wipes into the trunk of my jalopy. Luckily, the playpen folded up easily and fit alongside them. I filled the diaper bag from my baby shower with more diapers and wipes, another change of clothes for Zoe, and a few toys. Since I hadn't really gone anywhere since her birth, the tags were still on the bag. I pulled at the string of tags until it broke, leaving behind a small hole in the pastel fabric.

After emailing my uncle to tell him I was going on a trip, I set two of my houseplants, Dip and Dot, on the floor of the living room for him to easily water.

Zoe remained asleep as I placed her in the car seat, sliding the straps over her chubby arms and snapping the clasp in place. After finally installing the car seat last night, I noted how lonely it must feel to be stuck in a car, with only the boring fabric of the backseat to look at. Later while lying in bed beside Zoe, I had an idea. Grabbing her stuffed red and white giraffe from the nightstand, I eased my way off the mattress without waking her. I propped my pillow alongside her body while the giraffe and I made a trip to the kitchen.

Sliding the drawer underneath the pantry open, I grabbed the duct tape. It only took a minute to tape the smiling animal to the backseat. At least she would have something to look at during our road trip. Zoe slept for the first hour, but by hour two, she was done. Her screaming was making me tense, so I pulled the car into a brightly lit rest stop. After getting out of the car and quickly stretching my sore back, I opened the back door to get her out. As soon as I pulled the door open, she quieted and gave me a large gummy smile.

"You little faker." I laughed. She responded with a loud hiccup and another grin. Awkwardly, I changed her wet diaper in the backseat. *Those public restrooms are nasty.* Nevertheless, I had to go and doubted I could hold it for another two hours. Zoe wriggled as I placed her in the baby sling, wrapping its fabric around both of us until only her neck and head could be seen. A tuft of her fuzzy strawberry blonde hair tickled my chin as I stood back up and closed the car door.

Momentary blindness clouded my view as I opened the glass doors to the rest stop pavilion. I hadn't realized the sunlight outside was quite so dazzling until I stepped into the dim interior. Unlike rest stops I'd frequented in the past, this one was nearly empty. Its glossy tiled floors sparkled, drawing additional attention to the loneliness of the building. A handful of masked people were sprinkled throughout the space, most of them employees busy wiping down countertops and door handles. I followed the signs to the restrooms, patting down the fabric around Zoe to ensure she was still tucked safely in place. Thankfully, I could use the facilities without touching much of anything.

Scrubbing my hands under the freezing cold water,

I studied my face in the mirror. Mandated social quarantining had not been kind to me. My pale skin stood out against the dark fringe of bangs. Placing my hand against Zoe's back, I leaned closer to the mirror to study my eyes. Sometimes, I hated the color of them. A murky green blue, that often changed hue with my mood. I was unremarkable. My features were plain, my hair limp, my clothes too large and unflattering. Quickly turning to leave, I nearly bumped into a young woman who was rushing into the bathroom with a small child.

"Sorry!" she chirped, ushering the girl into the nearest stall. "Bathroom emergency." She claimed while slamming the stall door closed. I cringed inwardly at the deluge of germ-riddled thoughts as I exited the ladies' room. My stomach grumbled at the smell of fries while observing the few masked inhabitants at the food court. *Is it safe to eat fast food?* I remember seeing something on the news about how the virus couldn't survive in heat. *Let's hope the fries are hot enough*, I thought as I followed the six-foot markers on the floor.

Zoe squirmed against me as I ordered. Even though I wore a face mask, I still felt exposed. It was as if everyone who caught sight of us *knew* she wasn't mine. *Would this fear of being discovered ever go away?* After touchless paying by credit card, I pushed the glass doors open with my butt and blinked against the harsh sunlight. One hand rested under Zoe's in the sling, while the other awkwardly balanced iced tea and a now crumpled bag of fries and burger. After managing to unlock the car and set down my food, I pumped a large squirt of hand sanitizer into my palms, and rubbed vigorously. The stinging smell of alcohol assaulted my nose, and I stretched my hands away from Zoe's body, waiting for them to dry.

"Okay, pretty girl. I'm sorry, but I have to put you back in your seat. We still have a little way to go." Her sky-blue eyes studied mine, and she gave me a crooked grin. But she wasn't a fan of the car seat, and I knew this brief moment of silence wouldn't last.

"I'm sorry." I cooed to her again, unwrapping her from the sling and tucking her back into her seat. She responded with a squawk, followed by a piercing cry.

"I know. I know. Shh."

She ignored my plea as I strapped her in and returned to my seat. Fumbling for my phone, I opened my podcast player while she continued to scream. Scrolling through my favorite podcasts, I picked a new one I'd downloaded to my phone especially for this occasion. As soon as the familiar and nasally voice filled the car, Zoe quieted. I found his oddity amusing.

A few days ago at home, after putting Zoe down unsuccessfully for a nap, I switched on the radio, hoping for a distraction. After reading up on schedules and napping, I'd decided to try the "cry it out method." Although I loved Zoe's pattern of napping on me, it was making it difficult to actually get any work done during the day. Working on my laptop was impossible as her ever-growing body enveloped my arms. After binge-watching an embarrassing number of shows, I was feeling a bit guilty over my lack of productivity.

There wasn't much cleaning to do around the house; one of the perks of living tiny, but I still had to clock in a few hours of online work every day. Luckily, freelance writing was a flexible way to make a living.

The occasional work, paired with the remaining money that my father left me, covered my expenses. But, after the cost of my tiny house and all the unexpected bills accompanying it, my nest egg wasn't going to last much longer.

In my desperation to not have to listen to her crying, I switched on the old-fashioned radio in my kitchen. The wooden piece of furniture was initially an eyesore when I found it last year at a yard sale. Now it was one of my prized possessions. I had stripped down the wood and re-stained it a light brown. The original knobs that I thought were black were actually made of cooper. After scrubbing them with an old toothbrush, I was pleased with the results. The fiery red-head I'd purchased it from told me that it still worked, but it was still a pleasant surprise each time I turned it on.

As I reached out to turn the volume down, Zoe started to whine. As soon the annoying voice reached a quieter level, Zoe started crying again. I turned it up and was rewarded with her silence. Despite the program being louder than I would have liked, I often let the show permeate my house throughout the entirety of Zoe's nap. It had worked so well that I downloaded a bunch of episodes onto my phone and played them whenever she didn't want to fall asleep on her own. She hadn't been on many car rides since her arrival, but I was proud of myself for planning ahead and downloading a few new episodes for the trip. Even though the host's voice irked me, it was insightful and entertaining.

The rest of the ride was uneventful. Zoe slept for about half of the time. The other half was spent babbling and kicking at her toy giraffe. When she started to get fussy, I noticed the putrid smell of a dirty diaper and was glad to see we weren't that far from Aubrey's house.

Even though Zoe seemed fairly calm, I couldn't stand the smell any longer, and I didn't want her to get a diaper rash. As I pulled into the next rest stop, Zoe began to wail.

"Okay, baby girl. It's okay. Let's get you cleaned up." I cooed. She smiled up at me momentarily before continuing to howl. Her tiny face scrunching up humorously. Rather than donning a mask to go inside, I grabbed one of Zoe's blankets and spread it out on the backseat.

After unbuckling her and lifting her from her seat, I lay her down on the blanket. She wasn't happy with this makeshift space and kicked her legs as I tried to strip her down to change her. The air outside was cold, so I tried to work fast. The heat that had accumulated in the car quickly dissipated into the autumn air while Zoe continued to protest.

Working as rapidly as I could, I swore at the diaper wipes as they clumped together. My hands continued to pull bunches of them out of the plastic container as I cursed under my breath. Once she was finally clean, I squished her angry body back into the seat and closed the back door.

Staring at her for a moment through the hazy window, I turned to look around the nearly empty parking lot. A smattering of cars sat nearby. Only one other person appeared to be in the area. An old woman, dutifully wearing her mask, shuffled to her car. She cocked her head and turned toward me as Zoe continued to fuss. Unable to see the lower half of her face, I wondered if she was judging me or smiling in my direction. I had neglected to pull my mask on, so I smiled at her and gave a tiny wave. She nodded and continued to her car. According to my phone, I was only about twenty minutes from Aubrey's home. Zoe was probably hungry. Should I make her a bottle right now or wait until we arrive? I could just nurse her in the back seat. Since I started supplementing with formula, Zoe seemed to stay full longer. Luckily, she greedily gulped down whatever I offered.

I'd forgotten to pack plastic bags, so I glanced around the parking lot again before climbing back into the front seat. The old woman was already in her car. Since she was several spots away from me and not looking, I plopped the diaper onto the pavement, pushing it past the wheel and under my car with my foot. *So much for environmentalism.*

Feeling guilty, I sat back down in the front seat and pulled my door closed. Starting the car back up, I turned the heater and the stereo on. I popped in her favorite CD, and a soothing male voice filled the car as I squirted hand sanitizer onto my palms. Zoe loved this music, and I soon found myself singing along as I grabbed my thermos of warm water and began mixing up a small bottle of formula. Zoe's cries had thankfully died down to a whimper.

"It's coming, sweetie. Just one more minute." The interior of the car was warming quickly. Adding the warm water to her bottle of powdered milkiness, I shook it well and clambered back outside to squeeze my way into the backseat. Awkwardly, I pulled the door shut as I handed her the bottle. I'd started weaning Zoe off of breastmilk a few weeks earlier. Now I was down to breastfeeding her only once a day, right before bedtime. The rest of the time, she eagerly took a bottle of formula. She sucked it down in great big gasping gulps as though it would disappear before she could enjoy it fully. Within about a week of switching to formula, she surprised me one day by reaching up and holding the bottle herself.

"Oh! Look at you!" I'd remarked out loud. My heart swelled with pride at her new accomplishment. I'd read that this was a positive developmental milestone. Yet, a small part of me felt sad. She was no longer completely reliant on me.

I shook myself from the memory and watched her for another moment before returning to the front seat. Her eyes were closed as she devoured the bottle, making tiny contented murmurs. I opened the door quickly, trying not to let too much cold air in. Returning to my seat, I pulled out my phone and smiled to myself as I opened a text.

—*Who am I gonna stalk during my neighborhood walks now?*—

The cryptic text messages were coming daily now. Often accompanied by a silly GIF. Sometimes it was simply a —*Have a nice day.*—

Other times it became more of a dialogue. I embraced the non-threatening, getting-to-know-you kind of conversation. Admittedly, I was beginning to look forward to the texts, even though part of me still felt scared at letting someone get too close to me. My darkness might scare them away. Sighing, I responded.

—*Oh, I'm sure there are some other ladies in the area who would love for you to drop by.*—

He immediately replied. —*None as pretty as you.*—

I grinned and reopened the map on my phone, beginning to sing along with Zoe's music as I pulled back onto the highway.

Chapter Nine

A short while later, we pulled into Aubrey's driveway. Her greatly loved pickup was parked in front of me. Her bumper was plastered with so many stickers that I laughed at the absurdity of it. Unlike me, Aubrey had always been comfortable with making a statement wherever she went. I preferred to blend into the background of life while she embraced every opportunity to make her mark.

Before I could even open my door, she came bounding out to greet me. Then she abruptly stopped a few feet from the car and shouted my way.

"Oh my gosh, Willow! I can't believe you actually came! We're so excited you are here!" Even after I opened my door and stepped into the sunshine, she continued yelling.

"Do you want me to put a mask on? Can I see Zoe? How long can you stay? I'm so excited!" I laughed at her exuberance and approached her for a hug. *Are we allowed to hug? Maybe this was a big mistake. What if I'm exposing us, and now we are going to die?* We'd gone over our fears and the risks of joining each other's *bubble,* on the phone. Both Aubrey and Brian were healthy and wore masks when they were around other people. Zoe and I never went anywhere, so my guess was we were pretty low risk too.

"My guess is that if we're gonna be staying here,

there's no point in a mask." She squealed which resulted in a squawk from Zoe, followed by immediate crying.

"Oh no! I'm sorry. I didn't mean to scare her." She backed away from the car.

"It's okay. She's not quite used to seeing anyone other than me." *That's an understatement.*

Clucking and shushing, I quickly unbuckled Zoe as she raised her arms to me.

"Oh my God! She looks *just* like you!" She reached for her, and Zoe responded by burying her head into my shoulder.

"Don't take it personally," I responded after seeing a look of disappointment cross over Aubrey's face. "It just might take her a little bit to warm up to you, that's all."

"Okay." Aubrey genuinely looked crestfallen as she moved back to my door, leaning in to pop the trunk. "I'll grab some of your stuff now and send Brian out to get the rest later. He's at work, but he'll be back in time for dinner."

"Uh, okay. Maybe just grab the playpen from the trunk and the diaper bag from the back seat?"

Aubrey raised her eyebrows as she peered into the trunk, her eyes searching for which item to select. Clearly, she was not well-versed in baby accouterments.

"The big rectangular blue thing. Um, the playpen?"

I waited until she pulled out the unwieldy item to shift Zoe to my hip while we leaned in so I could grab my purse from the front seat.

"Come on in!" Aubrey was practically bouncing with excitement as she proceeded to the house with the unwieldy rectangle hitting her leg with each awkard step. We followed her into the house, where we were greeted by barking.

"Oh, I put Eve in her crate. I didn't want her to scare Zoe. I should probably let her out back before she pees out of excitement. Thank God for fences."

"Okay. I'm honestly not sure what she'll think of Eve. She's never even heard a dog bark before." Zoe was wide-eyed but silent as she took in the bohemian space. Eve matched the personality of the living room. Although I would never admit it to Aubrey, she was probably the ugliest dog I had ever seen. She was fairly small, about the size of a microwave. Her brownish blonde fur was coarse and wiry and didn't improve her looks in any way. And if dogs could have an underbite, hers was of epic proportions. But Aubrey loved her, so I kept my observations to myself.

"Should I let her out?" She stood staring at the crate.

"Sure. I think it'll be fine." Zoe's tiny fingers clung to my shirt as she continued to gaze around the room.

"Would you like something to drink? Or eat? Or, maybe, do you want to see your room?" Aubrey pulled her wild, flaming curls into a messy bun on the top of her head. Her brilliant red hair was still as beautiful as ever and prompted a spark of jealousy in my chest.

"Um, coffee would be great! Zoe will need her second nap in a bit, but since she dozed in the car, I'm not sure she will actually be tired for a while." Before I could say anything else, Aubrey disappeared into the kitchen. "Decaf or regular?" She yelled in my direction.

"Regular, please. Do you have any creamer?"

"Do I?" A moment later she bounded back into the

room awkwardly, holding four large bottles of flavored creamers against her chest.

"Oh, wow. Still addicted to creamer, I see." I laughed as I sat down, propping Zoe into a sitting position on my lap. The mulberry color of the cushion's fabric matched Zoe's shirt, giving the appearance of a baby bobblehead among the pillows. "Hmm. So many choices. I guess I'll try the chocolate chip cookie creamer? Thank you."

"My favorite!" She nodded and ducked back into the kitchen. Eve jumped up next to us and began licking my jacket. Her tiny tongue deposited wet imprints onto the faded fabric. Zoe erupted into laughter as I joined in.

"Is Eve bothering you?" She peeked her head into the entryway of the living room.

"No." I laughed, "it looks like Zoe likes her."

Aubrey returned to the living room with two steaming cups of coffee. Setting the larger of the mugs on the table closest to me, she held hers as she carefully sat at the other end of the couch. Zoe kept her eyes on Eve and giggled every few seconds.

"She's so beautiful, Willow! What a cutie! And her hair! It's so blonde!" This was code for *did you ever reconnect with the one-night-stand man?* I didn't take the bait.

"Oh, I almost forgot! We brought you a present! Will you hold her while I run back out to the car?"

"You think she'll let me?" Aubrey didn't wait for an answer before setting down her coffee and scooching her way across the couch to hold her arms out to Zoe. Zoe regarded her warily, scrunching up her nose adorably before turning her attention back to Eve. I plunked her in Aubrey's lap and ran back out to the car, opening the backdoor to pull one of my potted plants from its space on the floor. Originally it had been a gift from Angel. She'd brought it to my tiny house the day I moved in.

"It's called a Wandering Jew. At least that's what it used to be called. I think it's been given a new more 'PC' name now. I can never remember what it is, though." Angel laughed while setting the decorative pot on my countertop. *"It reminded me of you."* She giggled again as my eyebrows raised quizzically. *"Well, not the Jew part...just the wandering part."*

"Okay. Thank you?" I gently touched one of the red-green leaves.

"You're done wandering...so I was thinking, whenever you have a day when you're feeling down, you can just look at the plant and be reminded of how far you've traveled."

I'd somehow managed to keep the treasure alive, and it had grown so much since I'd moved it that I had given away a few cuttings. This one seemed to like its new home in the purple clay pot I'd found at a yard sale last year. I carried it back to the house and set it on the coffee table in front of Aubrey. Eve was gone, and there was a puddle on the floor by the table.

"How lovely! Thank you, Willow." She smiled up at me while I tried to think of something profound to say.

I should say something special, like about her friendship or something. I silently reprimanded myself for not being more verbally expressive. But the words felt lodged in my throat, so I swallowed them down, hoping the gift would speak for itself.

Zoe reached for me, and I scooped her up eagerly. She settled her face between my neck and shoulder as her tiny mouth opened in a yawn.

"How can you still be tired?" I asked Zoe. She replied by signing she wanted more milk.

"Milk? You just had a whole bottle!" I'd gotten used to conversing with Zoe. Aubrey looked up and watched the interaction silently.

"Do you mind if I warm up another bottle for her? She must be going through a growth spurt."

"Of course! What do you need? A special warmer or something?"

"Actually, if you hold her for a minute, I can put some fresh formula together." I waited until Aubrey stood then handed her Zoe and made my way into the kitchen. She wasn't happy as she squawked and began to cry. Aubrey followed me and began to pace around the kitchen with her, worriedly glancing at me as I worked quickly.

"What do I do?" Panic rose in her voice.

"I'm almost done. Maybe carry her back into the living room? Is Eve around?"

She practically ran to the back door and let Eve back inside. I observed Aubrey squatting down to Eve, bringing Zoe to her level. A giggle erupted as the tiny dog grabbed Zoe's sock and pulled it off. She held out her other foot, waiting to see if Eve would take the bait. When she didn't, Zoe erupted into heartbreaking sobs.

"Oh dear! Do you want to take her now?" A sense of urgency crept into her tone.

I nodded, setting the bottle down and taking Zoe, who quieted again immediately.

"Let me show you to your room. Can I help with

anything to get her settled?"

"Actually, I need to set up the playpen. It only takes a minute. Would you hold her again? I handed Zoe back to her and motioned for her to lead the way. The apparatus kept bumping into my thigh as I ungracefully followed her up the carpeted staircase, my feet sinking into the softness. As she opened the door at the end of the hallway, Eve appeared from out of nowhere, running ahead of us and jumping onto the pristine bed. Zoe's dramatic cries were replaced by a hiccupping laugh.

"Well, I think we can safely say she likes your dog."

I pulled on the arms of the playpen, flinging the miraculous makeshift bed out and locking it into place. Aubrey nodded while thrusting Zoe back into my arms.

"But I don't think she likes me all that much," she pouted.

"She's just tired. That was the longest car ride she's ever been on, and she's not a big fan of being stuck in the car seat."

"I'll let you get her settled. Do you need anything else?" Aubrey scooped Eve up and began backing away toward the door.

"Nope. I think we're okay for now. I'll come back down in a bit." Zoe and I sank into the cushiony rocker. She pulled the bottle from my hands and began to gulp greedily. Her eyes were already closing. The warmth of her tiny body and the rocking of the chair soothed both of us. I waited until the door clicked closed to nestle my face into her fluffy golden hair. Breathing in her milky apricot scent, I felt my body slowly let go of the slight awkwardness of the situation. Zoe snuggled into me, and I could feel myself becoming drowsy along with her. Before giving in to dozing off, I laid Zoe down and tiptoed out of the room.

Back downstairs, Aubrey was busy washing dishes. Her kitchen was cluttered, to say the least. The countertops housed a variety of appliances, including a toaster, coffee maker, microwave, spice rack, and several ceramic jars of assorted shapes and colors.

"Can I help you?" I moved closer to the sink, picking up a random towel from the drying rack.

"Oh, no need. I'm almost done. I do them in stages." She rinsed the fork in her hand and turned off the water. "Dishes are my most dreaded chore. So, I wash them piecemeal."

"Wouldn't it just be easier to do them all at once and get it over with?" A flash of a memory popped into my head of Mrs. Calkins dumping a stack of food-crusted dishes into the large, stained sink. Anyone who hadn't finished every bit of food on their plates was not allowed to have dessert. She had been so adamant about each of us eating every morsel of food at dinner she would only allow dessert if our plates were clean enough to turn over and eat it off the back of the plate. The problem was that she was a horrible cook. Boiled chicken, off-brand hotdogs, and government cheese were staples in our house. Pairing that with powdered milk seemed to take every morsel of enjoyment out of meals. Needless to say, most of us never managed to get dessert. I shook the memory away, turning my attention back to Aubrey.

"Thanks again for inviting us to stay with you. Are you sure Brian doesn't mind?"

"No, not at all. It'll give you a chance to get to

know him a bit better, and I couldn't pass up an opportunity to meet Zoe in person! No offense, but I'm kind of burned out from online meetings." She laughed. "Once Covid is finally over, we won't remember how to actually interact with other humans in person! Ya know?"

"I know what you mean. I wasn't going out much before Covid hit. Honestly, as horrible as things are right now, it's been a blessing for my social anxiety." Even as the words tumbled out of my mouth, I could feel the guilt creeping in. How could I even hint that there was anything positive to come from this deadly pandemic when so many lives have been lost? Before I could admonish myself further, a thump overhead interrupted us. I ran up the stairs and flung open the guest bedroom door, mentally bracing myself for tragedy. Zoe was fast asleep. The now empty bottle beside her chubby hand.

"Is she okay?" Aubrey whispered from behind me.

I nodded, holding a finger up to my lips. Aubrey smiled and turned back toward the hallway. I followed her in silence, easing the door partially closed. Suddenly Eve bounded down the hall. She abruptly stopped in front of Aubrey's feet, proudly dropping a wad of white and red onto the floor.

"What the hell?" Aubrey bent to take a closer look. After a few seconds, we both recognized the wadded-up maxi pad wrapped in toilet paper. "Oh my God, Eve!" Aubrey bent and scooped the offending wad into her hand. "That's disgusting! I'm so sorry." Her face now scarlet, she quickly popped into the bathroom while I remained in the hallway feeling awkward and embarrassed for her. Should I just go ahead and walk back downstairs? I could hear her moving around in the bathroom. I moved back to the doorway of the guest bedroom and watched Zoe sleep. Her tiny body was barely visible in the dim light of the room.

"I'm sorry you had to see that," Aubrey whispered as she made her way back down the hallway. "I even got a new trash can with a lid in there. She somehow managed to get it open again. Ugh."

"Don't worry about it," I whispered in return, trying to make my voice sound nonchalant and light.

"How long will she sleep?" Aubrey proceeded to walk back down the stairs, and I took that as my opportunity to follow.

"Probably another hour and a half or so."

As we neared the bottom of the stairs, I could hear a tiny beeping noise.

"Oh my gosh! My muffins! I forgot all about them!" Aubrey rushed into the kitchen, grabbed her oven mitts, and threw the oven door open. The beeper continued to buzz, so I leaned over to turn it off. The room smelled heavenly, like blueberry and vanilla. Its warmth drew me in as I plunked down on a kitchen chair.

"Are they okay?"

"Surprisingly, yeah. The timer must have just gone off. They look just right."

"When did you even put muffins together?" I laughed.

"Oh, I had the batter in the fridge, and I just stuck it in the oven when you were putting Zoe down for her nap."

"Wow. You're a regular jailbait cook extraordinaire," I joked.

"Hardly. Most of the time, we order take-out. I'm kind of a horrible cook. So is Brian. But I do like to bake," she said, patting the extra layer surrounding her middle.

"Well, you're in luck because I do like to eat!" I snickered.

"They need a few minutes to cool down. Want to go sit in the living room for a bit?"

"Sure," I said, standing back up.

"Can I get you more coffee or tea?"

"No thanks. I'm still working on my cup from earlier. I think I left it on the table by the couch." I followed her back into the living room and grabbed my mug as I settled against her fluffy white pillows. "Aub, I don't want you to feel like you have to entertain me or bake for us, or whatever. I mean, I'm sure you have stuff to do."

"Like what?" Her voice rose in amusement. "I took the week off from work. No one is going to miss me at the library."

"How's that going anyway? I mean, since Covid hit?" My phone buzzed, and I tried to ignore the desire to check my texts. Despite my pocket vibrating and my heart rate increasing, I kept my focus on Aubrey.

"Oh, not bad. I mean, I mostly just fill online orders for patrons who want to come pick up a bunch of stuff. There are still a lot of people signing things out of the library. We just put orders together and bring them out to their cars."

I nodded toward the stack of library books piled up on one of her side tables. I pushed the intrusive thought about germ-infested books out of my mind. "I see you have your own stash."

"Yeah, it's one of the ways I procrastinate cleaning while Brian is off at work. But enough about that. Tell me what's been going on with you? I mean, you have a freaking *baby*! What was the labor like? Was it horrible? Were you going crazy in your little house during lockdown? Do you like being a mom?"

"Slow down," I said, laughing at her exuberance.

Thankfully, I had prepared myself well during the drive down here. I knew there would be questions, and I wanted to make sure my story made sense. Even though Aubrey was my closest friend, there were still things I could never tell her.

"I love being a mom. I've always wanted a baby for as long as I can remember. It's an exhausting but amazing experience. But, I highly recommend it." Raising my eyebrows comically I gave her a goofy grin. "Have you and Brian thought about starting a family?"

"I see what you're doing, and I promise we will go there, but first, I want to hear more. Tell me all the juicy details. Did you ever reconnect with the one-night-stand guy? Does he know about Zoe?"

"No. And I'm fine with that. It really was a one-time thing. I know it must make me sound like a floozy, but I didn't even know his last name. I'm happy raising her on my own."

"Really?"

"Really. And the labor wasn't bad. I mean, it wasn't a walk in the park, but it was fast. I actually ended up delivering her at home."

"What? How could I not know that? You delivered her at home? Like with a midwife or something? How very modern of you." Aubrey stood and grabbed her mug from the side table. "I want to hear the rest of this story, but my coffee is cold. I hate cold coffee. Unless, of course, it's *iced* coffee. In which case, it's meant to be cold. Then I like it. With lots of creamer," she added. "I'll be right back. Can I top you off?"

I flipped over my phone, which lay on the cushion beside me. It was nearing three p.m., which meant If I had any more caffeine, I wouldn't sleep well later tonight. As it was, I felt nervous about sleeping anywhere other than my comfortable bed at home.

"Thanks, but I'd better not."

"Okay, be right back." She scrambled off to the kitchen while I peeked at the newest text.

—Hey beautiful, did you make it there ok?—

I smiled and resisted the urge to reply. I wanted to wait until I had more time to text back. I began to scroll through my phone. Social media was a rabbit hole I often fell down willingly. Although I didn't have hundreds of *friends*, there was always a plethora of lives to virtually explore. The glossy, smiling photos of beautiful people flaunting their adventures drew me in. Of course, since Covid hit, most of the *adventures* were limited to home renovations and art projects, but it was still an alluring glimpse into other people's lives. Before I could stalk any further, Aubrey returned.

"Sorry. Now, please tell me all the gory details."

"Well, I was supposed to deliver her at the hospital, but everything happened so fast I didn't have time to get there."

"I thought labor usually took like, thirty-six hours or some crazy shit like that."

"I mean, I guess it can. But not for me. I woke up one morning with cramping, kind of like period cramps, but way worse. When I climbed down from my loft, my water broke. So, I tried to clean that up, but the cramping got worse. It felt like a huge rubber band was tied around my entire torso and was squeezing me tight. I knew I couldn't drive, and I was going to call for a car, but before I knew it, I just started to feel like I had to push."

"Oh my God, this is amazing! So, you were there by yourself?"

"Yep. I managed to grab some towels and stuff, and then I just got into the tub. Before I knew it, there she was."

"Holy cow! That's crazy! Wasn't it a mess? I didn't even know you had a tub in that tiny bathroom." Aubrey's face was scrunched into a look of amazed disgust.

"Yeah, it was pretty disgusting. I ended up throwing those towels out. But the overall clean-up was surprisingly easy. And, it's not like a full 'tub', more like a large shower floor with short walls. It's just enough room to sit scrunched up in." I laughed, even though a part of me felt sad. I pushed the image of my son's still form from my mind.

"Oh my God. That is unbelievable! How did you know what to do? Were you scared?"

"I dunno, my body just seemed to know what to do. I didn't have time to be scared until after. I guess my endorphins…"

"Shh. Is that Zoe?" Aubrey looked up at the ceiling as if she could see through it. Zoe was babbling happily. She might need to be changed. Usually, she woke up babbling, but if it continued and grew louder, she wouldn't be falling back asleep. At least I had a diversion from the rest of my story for now.

"I'll run up and check. She might fall back asleep after I change her. She's been taking these micro naps recently. So, I might be up there rocking her for a bit."

"Okay, I'll catch up on some junk TV." She grabbed the remote and clicked the TV on. "Don't judge me," she yelled as I climbed the stairs.

To say Zoe had pooped would be an understatement. Somehow her entire back was covered. It was as if her diaper had exploded, leaving behind a disgusting trail of terror. Zoe didn't seem all that bothered by the event. She stood, with her pudgy fingers reaching for me as I surveyed the best tactic to attack this biological hazard.

"Um, Aubrey?" I yelled, hoping my voice carried downstairs. "Mind if I put Zoe in the bath?" I grabbed a tissue from the box on the nearby dresser, ripping off a strip and plugging each nostril. My eyes watered from the toxic emission.

I could hear Aubrey thumping back up the stairs. She was winded as she stood in the doorway with her hand pressed up against her nose. "Holy cow! How can such a little thing produce such a stink?"

"I know, right?" I grimaced as I held the poop monster at arm's length while carrying her to the bathroom.

"Hey Aub," I yelled. "Would you mind grabbing me a clean diaper and a onesie for her? They're in the green and yellow diaper bag."

Aubrey erupted into laughter when she came into the bathroom. Zoe was precariously perched on the side of the tub with my arm around her while I fiddled with the spouts, haphazardly adjusting the water temperature. Always afraid of accidentally scalding my precious child, the water switched from tepid to frigid.

"Can I give you a hand?" Without waiting for a response, she leaned over me to take care of the water, while I began peeling the poop covered clothing off of Zoe. A clump of tissue plopped from my nose onto the floor. The putrid smell immediately offended my open nostril.

"Um, do you have a bag I could put this in?" I held the encrusted clothing between two fingers as I pushed the wadded tissue toward the garbage can with my foot.

"Here," she said, flinging a hand towel to the floor, "just set it on this. I can throw a load of laundry in later. Eve threw up on my comforter earlier, so I'll just throw it all in together."

"You're a saint." I threw Zoe's clothes onto the towel, where they landed with a soft plop.

"Thank you so much! Sorry to cause such trouble."

Zoe squealed as I set her in the now warm water. She loved bath time. Tiny specks of dried excrement began to fleck off her back into the water. There was no good way of doing this.

"Could I borrow a big cup from you?" I was beginning to worry we were already wearing out our welcome. And we'd only been here a few hours so far.

"Sure. I'll be right back." Aubrey scooped up the literal pile of shit and zipped out as I unclogged the drain, hoping to dispel some of the brown remnants down. Moving Zoe out of harm's way, I carefully turned the faucet on again, hoping to replace the dingy water.

Aubrey returned with a large plastic tumbler, which I thankfully accepted.

"You don't have to stay here." I glanced over at her

as she pulled the top of her sweater up over her nose.

"Are you sure you don't need any help?"

"I got this, but thanks."

****

After successfully bathing Zoe and getting her into fresh clothes, I debated putting her back down to finish her nap. She might fall back asleep, but at this rate, if she did so, her nighttime schedule would be off. Envisioning an evening sipping wine with Aubrey in front of the fireplace prompted me to carry Zoe back downstairs with me.

"Better?" Aubrey asked from the comfort of her couch. A contented Eve was snoring away at her side.

"Much, thanks. I'm gonna try to keep Zoe up for a while so she'll sleep better tonight. What time does Brian come home?"

"Usually by six. He says he'll be home around four thirty, but that usually means six." She shrugged. *Was that a bit of resentment I heard in her voice? I'd have to ask her more about Brian later tonight, after a few glasses of wine.*

"Can I help with dinner or anything? I don't want you to feel like you have to change your schedule because of us."

"Nope. I threw some chili in the crockpot. We should be good to go. Besides, I took the whole week off. I'm at your disposal." She paused and offered a dramatic bow., "Not that there's much we can do right now anyway. I can't wait until life can return to normal."

I set Zoe on the floor. She crawled over to Aubrey's feet and sat on them, all the while staring at Eve as if she was a plate of cookies.

"Well, hello." Aubrey reached down and lifted Zoe onto her lap. Zoe squealed in delight as she grabbed a handful of Eve's fur. Quickly I leaned over, placing my hand over Zoe's and lightly pushing down so she wouldn't hurt the dog.

"Gentle, Zoe." I placed my other hand on Eve's back and began to stroke her slowly. "Gentle. Don't pull. You don't want to hurt her." Zoe loosened her grip as she watched me. She had grown so much in the past few months. According to the birthday I'd given her, she would now be nearing nine months old. I looked out the front window at the snow-covered lawn. It was snowing so lightly that it was hardly perceptible. I hated this time of year. So close to spring, yet most of the days so far were still frigid and snowy. Knowing I didn't have to go back out in it helped me appreciate its beauty even more. Winter has always been my least favorite season.

"So I was thinking that while you're here, I could show you around town a bit." I looked up at Aubrey with raised eyebrows. "I mean, we would wear masks and everything. And only go to places with limited crowds."

"I dunno, Aub," I said, grabbing Zoe's pudgy fingers before they could clasp onto the dog's fur. "I don't want to expose Zoe to anything. I mean, there's still so much we don't know about this virus. What if it really is airborne? I literally haven't taken Zoe anywhere since her birth. Even if we didn't have this virus to worry about, she's only been exposed to me."

"Yeah, I know. I guess I'm just eager to get out. I feel like I'm going a bit crazy." She picked a piece of link from her shirt and flicked it onto the floor. I tried to ignore it as she continued.

"Brian gets to go to the office sometimes. But I'm stuck here all day."

"You don't like being home?" I'd always relished the peace and comfort of being alone. No one to entertain. No need to converse. Of course, now that Zoe was in the picture, my life had changed dramatically.

"I know, I know. I'm lucky to be able to work from home. I'm not trying to complain. Brian wishes he could work from home every day. His boss is still making him come in a few times a week. He's so scared of getting sick. When he gets home, he strips in the garage and heads right to the shower. This whole thing is so nerve-wracking."

"It is. How about we take Zoe for a walk?" A walk in the cold was about the last thing I wanted to do, but since Aubrey was being nice enough to let us stay over, I felt like I should humor her.

Chapter Ten

Do you think I should change the name of the church again? I mean, what if it's still too close to the real name and someone from my old life reads the book? Not that they would. But still. Maybe I could just publish this in Canada or something? LOL. My therapist says I should look at why I care what people who are no longer part of my life think of me. What would that even feel like? -W

I didn't want to like Mrs. Stevens, but I couldn't help myself. Rather than dreading our ever-expanding church services, I began looking forward to my time there. After all, the church had become my second home. I was there every weekday for school, as well as worship services on Wednesday, Friday, and Sunday nights. But Sunday mornings were becoming my least favorite. Earlier this morning, Mrs. Calkins brought me in to see Pastor Mettin. As we approached the door to his office, I could feel my stomach cramping in protest. Being called into the pastor's office was a big deal. His office was adjacent to the sanctuary, and I'd heard there was even a special door in his paneled wall that led to the area behind the pulpit.

Mrs. Calkins placed her hand on my shoulder as

we climbed the lushly carpeted steps to his entrance. Standing outside the double-stained glass doors, I noticed even the carpet up here was different. It was a lighter color blue than the carpet in the main foyer of the church. My feet sank into the unfamiliar plush. Before we could knock, the door swung open, and the pastor's personal secretary greeted us.

"Hi, Willow. Pastor is ready to see you. He only has a few minutes, so ahead in."

My body froze as I turned to look at Mrs. Calkin. Wasn't she going to come in with me? She pushed me forward,

"Now, Willow, don't be shy. Pastor won't bite!" Her hearty laugh faded as the secretary took my hand and led me into the inner sanctum. The room was enormous. Despite his six-foot frame, Pastor Mettin looked small behind his huge mahogany desk. Several well-cushioned chairs were placed throughout the room. The two largest chairs were closer to me on the other side of his desk. Who needed this many living room chairs in an office? I looked around at the stained-glass windows as he stood to greet me. The light streaming through each pane left the room dim, casting strange shadows along the walls.

"W-Willow." He cleared his throat. "Just the girl that I wanted to see. Would you like to sit down?" He motioned to the high-backed velvet chair beside him. My special "church shoes" felt glued to the floor as I placed my hand on the arm of the chair beside me and moved to sit down there.

"Come on over here," he said, stretching out his meaty hands toward me. I hesitated but obeyed. He waited until I was seated closer to him to return to his chair.

"Now, I called you in today because I hear you are interested in Bible camp."

I nodded but remained silent.

"G-good, good," he continued. "Excellent. We would like you to be able to go, but as you may know, camp can be a bit pricey."

I tried to keep my eyes focused on his plump face but found myself scanning the room for the hidden door.

"The church would like to pay for you to be able to attend Bible camp this summer." He paused, waiting for a response. "Is this something you'd would like to do?"

I nodded again.

"You're so shy." He chuckled. "That's all right. We seem to have quite a few shy children at this church. Okay then, I just wanted to meet with you to let you know we will make it possible for you to go away to camp this summer." He paused, staring at me until I spoke up.

"Thank you." My stomach felt as if a dozen butterflies were trapped within.

He laughed again. But this time, it sounded tight and low.

"Wonderful! Then, that is all for now, Willow."

I stood quickly, ready to leave this strange space and its murky interior. Before I could step away, his hand reached out and grabbed my arm. He held tight as I stood as still as a doe caught in the forest.

"What do you say, Willow?" His grip on my arm tightened just a bit.

"Thank you, Pastor. Thank you." I cautiously smiled up at him as my heart raced.

"W-Wonderful. I'm happy to make this happen for you. You are going to have an amazing time this summer. When you get back, I'll expect a full report as to how it went."

I held my breath as I waited for his grip to lessen. If only I could spot the hidden door and run through it, I thought.

"Now, may I give you a hug?" He raised his eyebrows slightly and let go of my arm to extend his arms in my direction. A hug from Pastor? I felt like it was the last thing I wanted to do, but I stepped forward into his awkward embrace. The butterflies inside of me were swarming, flittering against the interior of my chest. He pulled me close, my head aligned with his massive stomach. Placing a hand on top of my head, he made a declaration.

"And now, may the blood of Christ wash over this child. Protecting and guiding closer and ever more closer to the truth. Amen."

As he let go, I hurried to the door and turned to offer him an obligatory smile. I pushed the door open and stepped into the familiar energy of the foyer. The secretary and Mrs. Calkins greeted me.

"All set then, Willow?"

I nodded as Mrs. Calkins placed her hand on my shoulder again and guided me away from the inner sanctum toward the nursery. I could hear the choir practicing in the sanctuary as I approached the nursery door.

"Isn't it exciting?" Mrs. Calkins asked. "Pastor was kind enough to offer to pay for you to attend Bible camp this summer! We must always remember to be thankful for God's blessings. We are indebted to Pastor

Mettin for his generosity."

"Yes, thank you." I numbly repeated as I turned the knob to enter the nursery.

"All right then, I'll see you after the service." Mrs. Calkins walked away.

****

April 12, 2021

By the time Brian got home from work, I was a bit tipsy. After the first few weeks of nursing Zoe, she began to lose interest in breast milk. Although she was now mostly on formula, I had held off on drinking. Drinking alone in a tiny house just felt way too pathetic to me. But when Aubrey offered me some pre-dinner wine, I gave in. It probably didn't help that I hadn't had enough to eat all day. So, when we sat down to dinner, I dug in right away. Zoe was balanced on my lap and kept reaching for my food. Although she was still too young for table food, after several seconds of ear-piercing squeals of protest, I gave in and presented her with a plain roll to hold onto. She delighted in gumming the bread until it became an unrecognizable soggy mess.

"Can I help you clean up?" I tried to offer Zoe to Brian so I could help clear the table. His gaze was one of a deer in headlights, so I settled back down with Zoe on my lap.

"No worries, you've got your hands full. I cook. He does the dinner dishes." Aubrey grinned as she poked Brian with a dirty spoon. She reached across the table and began pushing all of the plates in his direction.

"Yep, she's got me trained," he joked as he stood and began clearing the table.

It felt awkward to just sit and watch them clean, so I scooped Zoe up and tried to grab a few glasses to carry to the kitchen.

"Really, we've got it." Aubrey shooed me away. I picked up Zoe, and I followed Eve out into the living room. She clung to me as we walked around the space, stopping at the bookshelf. I glanced at the titles, noting the collection of Willa Cather books. Scrolling through the titles, I looked over her collection, my gaze stopping at the ugly monkey statue that was propping up the lowest stack of books.

"Oh my gosh, I can't believe you still have Mr. Binkey!"

Zoe reached for him as I picked the small statue up with my free hand. Mr. Binkey stood about half a foot tall, his wood faded from the years of sun and occasional dust. I rubbed my thumb across the monkey's snub nose. Most of him was dark brown. His carefully carved black eyes still seemed to sparkle, despite their age. He wore a tailored red suit with small gold buttons down the front. I flipped him over to confirm my memory of his outfit was correct. A tiny hole allowed for his carved tail to poke out of the back of his coat. Its tip curled around one of his black shoes.

Suddenly, Eve came bounding past us. She was dragging a large and very tattered stuffed bear. I imagined at one time it was white. Violently, she whipped it back and forth, shaking it with her mouth while growling. Zoe began to whimper as I backed away from the bookshelf to watch.

"Oh, yeah. I couldn't get rid of Mr. Binkey!" Aubrey came into the living room with two refilled glasses of wine. I was going to have to pump and dump later. Maybe this was a good time to fully give up breastfeeding.

"Trust me, I tried to get rid of that ugly old thing, but she wouldn't let me." Brian chuckled from the kitchen. I could hear the dishes clanking in the sink.

"Once I told him *you* gave it to me, he stopped pestering me about it. You gave me Mr. Binkey at the eighth grade field day." Aubrey set the goblets down on the coffee table. "After I lost the relay race."

"Well, clearly, *you* should have won. Cindy Mastrioni's boobs should have slowed her down. And you were so crushed to have lost." I clucked my tongue as I made my way over to the couch. After setting Zoe on the floor with some throw pillows, I nudged the wine glasses further away from her reach and sat beside Aubrey.

"It was the first thing that I ever stole. I had it hidden in the bottom of my backpack, so Mrs. C wouldn't find it."

"Oh, that's right!" Aubrey reached for her wine and took a sip. "I totally forgot Mr. Binkey was the beginning of your five-finger-discount phase!"

"Oh, so you're a klepto, huh?" Brian was still drying his hands as he came into the living room. I tried not to think about the germs lingering on the towel as he tossed it to the arm of the couch. He squatted to pull the bear from Eve, who barked in return. I picked at a cutical.

"What's with that ugly old bear anyway?" I asked.

"Humpy Bear," they replied in unison.

"Humpy bear? Why?"

"You'll see." Their voices merged again.

Chapter Eleven

To: Melaniewalker@catharsistimepress.com
From:Willowmorgan666@gmail.com
Subject: age 12
*Mel, This was my least favorite Christmas. Oh,
well. It only gets better from here, right? My therapist
says that since I've lived through so much crap, I
should allow myself to find enjoyment wherever I can.
I'm not sure that's the best approach. I mean, look at
all the people suffering around the world right now.
Why would I deserve joy when so many people are in so
much pain? Is joy something we earn? Ugh. Sorry for
the rant. Here's the next chapter. -W*

As foster kids, we always seemed to have less than
everyone else. Still, I was looking forward to Christmas
this year. Creeping down the old wooden staircase, I
skipped the 6th step to avoid the squeaky spot. The
artificial tree looked pretty in a chintzy way. Its fake
branches decorated with homemade ornaments that all
of us kids had worked on. I made my way over to the
unlit tree to look for my favorite ornament. I pulled the
tiny clothespin angel from the tree to study her again.
Her clothespin body was decorated with a crudely
scribbled blue "gown." Her beady black eyes were
faded dots of magic marker. Although much of her
celestial being was worn away, her red lips remained a
perfect red bow. I flipped her over and rubbed my

thumb over the barely legible scribbled name, Katie. My first Christmas with the Calkins was three years ago. I remember asking about Katie, hoping for a dramatic story. But Mrs. C brushed my curiosity aside by simply answering that Katie had been a foster kid who only stayed for a few months. I traced the angel's paltry head as I wondered about Katie's outcome. Why was she put in foster care anyway? Did she return to her family? Where was she now?

My curiosity was intercepted by Mr. C.

"What are you doing up so early?" He asked from the room's entry.

"Oh, I couldn't sleep."

"Excited about Christmas, I see." He walked over to the tree, bending to plug the lights in.

"Yeah, I guess." I tried to play it cool. Show him that I wasn't too eager for selfishly wanting presents.

"Christmas is such a profound remembrance." He sat on the couch. My gaze settled on the leather-bound Bible in his hand. Had he brought it in with him? How many massive Bibles did he actually have?

"The birth of our Lord and Savior, Jesus Christ."

I nodded mutely.

"'And she brought forth her firstborn son, and wrapped him in swaddling clothes, and laid him in a manger; because there was no room for them in the inn. Luke chapter 2, verse 7,'" he quoted.

After waiting for another nod from me, he closed his eyes and began speaking in tongues. Speaking in tongues had been such a bizarre occurrence when I first observed it. Now, it was the norm. Apparently, in the world of a born-again charismatic Christians, once you were baptized by water in a *spirit-filled* church, God might bless you with the gift of tongues. In our church, speaking in tongues was a sort of rite of passage. If you had already said The Sinner's Prayer, attended a special Catechism class, and been baptized, you might someday be given the *Gift of Tongues.*

Basically, this meant God would give you a special language that only He understood. It was known as a way for your spirit to speak directly to God without the interruption of any known language. Not only did it seem plain old crazy to me, but what added to the confusion was that according to the Bible, if someone spoke out loud in tongues, God would give another believer the Gift of Prophecy. This *Gift* was one of translating the mouthful of syllables into a concrete message that we could then understand. Both options seemed terrifying to me, and I didn't want to be given either of those gifts.

"*Hahdehacki Lochimobie Wallam,*" he began. "*Wallam Chuchi Sheedo. Phfuntnut Callakecki. Wallam phfuntnut callekecki.*" He repeated some semblance of this phrase about twenty more times. Finally, he paused and inhaled deeply. His eyes remained closed. The Bible he was clutching was beginning to slip from his grip. I wondered what he would do if I snuck out of the room while he was praying. It wasn't worth taking the risk as I assumed her would see that as disrespectful in some way and worthy of punishment. I stared at the lights on the tree and wished I had stayed in my room a bit longer.

"Oh Lord, dear Lord. How wonderful is thy name, oh Lord. Although we are poor in gifts, we are rich in spirit. We remember to be generous with all that thou hast wrought unto us. And to deliver unto others that which You have blessed us with. In the name of Jesus. Amen."

I became aware of my slack mouth stance. So I righted myself and stood up straight as he opened his eyes.

"No gifts this year, Willow. Our Lord God has spoken. We must bless those less fortunate with this abundance." He declared as he swept his hand over our stack of Christmas gifts.

My stomach began swirling with nervous energy. What was he saying?

"Go wake up your brothers and sisters." His gaze held mine. "We have to pack up these gifts and prepare to give them to a less fortunate family.

****

To say I was baffled by the idea God had somehow declared to Mr. C that we give away our Christmas gifts was an understatement. All of us kids had a hard time believing that God would pick a bunch of underprivileged foster kids' Christmas gifts to share with those even less fortunate.

"It's not fair." Molly sobbed as I rubbed her back and handed her pieces of one-ply toilet paper for her nose.

"Aren't we already the *poor* family of the church? Who are we supposed to find to give our gifts to?"

It was no secret that our family was considered the poorest in our church. When your whole life had been supplied with handouts, there was no room left for shame. In fact, when our weekly brown bags of groceries were dropped off by a church volunteer, we had a bit of a celebration. Brand-name cereal was a luxury! One time the food was delivered when Molly and I were the only ones home. The package of individually boxed cereals was too tempting to resist. We tore into each tiny box of cereal, tasting each brand-named flavor. Meticulously, we folded the waxy paper back in place and neatly stacked the colorful boxes in the pantry. When Mrs. C got home from her afternoon prayer service, she called us downstairs to the kitchen.

"Girls. Did you open these boxes of cereal?"

Molly and I stared at her, silent and remorseful.

"Well?" She pressed. "You may want to think before speaking, girls. Jesus is always watching. He sees you all the time. Even when you think no one is looking."

Molly started to cry. We both knew what was going to happen. Any sin, no matter how small, was corrected by spanking. Mrs.C's gaze flicked to the belt hanging on the nail next to the fridge.

"We will discuss this further when your father gets home," she said. "For now, go to your room. I want each of you to find a Bible verse that speaks to your act of deceit. Then I want you to get your notebooks and write down that verse one hundred times. When you are done, you may leave your notebooks on your father's desk.

"Yes, ma'am," I whispered as a silent Molly followed me back to our room to await our fate.

Chapter Twelve

April 12, 2021

Zoe's eyes were getting heavy. We usually have a very specific bedtime routine, including bath time and stories. I was still feeling a bit tipsy, so I carefully carried Zoe upstairs to the portable playpen I'd brought. She settled quickly with her favorite blanket and her stuffed rabbit. I clicked on lullabies I'd downloaded and switched my phone to airplane mode so it wouldn't accidentally ring and wake her. Not that many people ever bothered to call me. Tiptoeing out of the room, I left the door ajar so I could hopefully hear her from downstairs if she needed me. I rarely used the baby monitor I'd gotten as a gift, as our house was so small I could easily hear her from anywhere.

"She's down for the count." I returned to the living room, setting a clear plastic container with a bright red lid onto the coffee table.

"What's that?" Aubrey sat up from her lounging position and scooched to the edge of the couch to get a closer look.

"I made you guys some peanut butter fudge." I eased the lid open, listening to the satisfying hiss it made as the air escaped. "Just a little gesture of thanks for having us over in the middle of all of this craziness."

"We were glad you could come. Thank you." Brian reached out to take a piece of the fudge.

"Oh my god, Willow. This is amazing!" Aubrey sank her teeth into another bite.

"Thanks. So how have things been for you guys during the past year? I mean like, what about your jobs? Are they pretty secure? Do you know anyone who's had Covid?"

"Thankfully, both of our jobs have been saved. We were lucky to be able to do a lot of our work online. Brian only has to go into the store once or twice a week." Aubrey licked the tip of her thumb and forefinger. I felt myself bristle at the thought of the germs from her skin she just willingly ingested. *Maybe I should go wash my hands again. Who knows how dirty the hand railing is. Did I touch it on my way down?*

I pushed the thought away, reminding myself that I had no control over her germ intake. *I could either go wash my hands again, or skip touching the fudge. Maybe I could grap a piece with a tissue? There was a box nearby. That might look crazy though. Well, I didn't need fudge anyway.*

One of the many therapists I'd had over the years taught me a visualization to do when intrusive thoughts popped into my head.

1) Notice the thought and recognize it as intrusive.

2) Imagine placing the thought on a whiteboard, for example, drawing the word (germs), or a symbol or picture representing the intrusive thought.

3) Imagine yourself wiping the word away with a large eraser.

4) Repeat if necessary.

Repeat. Repeat. Repeat.

I had dozens of intrusive thoughts every day. Not only about germs but catastrophes. They'd seemed to have gotten worse since Zoe came along. In fact, the solitude of the past few months seemed to make the thoughts worse. Instead of simply imagining my car careening off the highway during a routine drive to the market, my brain was flooded with images of someone breaking into my tiny house and stealing Zoe. Or perhaps a mass shooting would occur at the exact moment I ventured to a gas station to fill up the tank. My brain was full of worst-case scenarios. Me, suddenly ill with a terminal disease, dying and leaving Zoe alone. Her, growing up in foster care. Lather, rinse, repeat.

"Willow?" Aubrey nudged my arm with her wine glass.

"What? Oh sorry. I kinda zoned out there for a minute." I grinned at the pair and cleared my throat. "Brian, what is it you do again? You're able to work mostly from home now? Cool." *Can they tell I'm beyond buzzed? Keep the conversation going, Willow. You've got this.*

"Yeah. I'm the guy behind the scenes that makes sure everything is ordered in time to keep the shelves fully stocked."

"Do you like it? You've been there a while, right?"

"It's a job. I mean the company is great. The benefits are great. I mean, it's not exactly my dream job, but I can't complain."

Leaning forward, I poured myself another swing of wine and winked at Brian.

"What *is* your dream job?" *Was I flirting with my*

best friend's husband? I studied Aubrey's face for signs of discomfort, but found none. Alcohol always seemed to not only loosen my inhibitions, but it made me like myself better. I felt more confident, less neurotic, and much more outgoing. It was one of the reasons I didn't drink much. I could see how tempting it would be to fall into drinking often and relying on this improved version of myself to get through life.

"I've actually been thinking about going back to school," he said.

"Brian wants to be a therapist." Aubrey stretched her legs over his on the couch. He began automatically rubbing her feet. "He'd make a great one. He's always listening to me talk about my feelings and crap like that, "she giggled.

"Ooh, I would make a fascinating case study for you, Brian." I tucked my legs underneath me and pulled a fluffy pillow onto my lap. "I'm a hot mess." I tried to keep my voice light, but the reality of my statement sat like a stone in my chest.

Aubrey regarded me for a moment. She knew my shit, and I could tell she was planning her words carefully.

"When you told me you were moving to a tiny house, I was a bit surprised at first. I mean, it makes sense. You've never really had a chance to live alone. So I was happy for you. But part of me also felt very sad."

"Why?" This surprised me. Aubrey grew up an only child. Her imagination was vivid and colorful, and even as kids, she would create amazing worlds for us to escape into. In high school, she turned her bedroom interior into a makeshift treehouse. Nestled in her extra-large hammock between two wooden trees she built with her father, we would lay side by side and talk long into the night. The twinkle lights strung throughout the fake leaves guided our discussions. In all my years of knowing Aubrey, she had almost never seemed sad about anything.

"Being alone can be great. But it can be lonely too. Haven't you been lonely?"

"I have Zoe," I interjected quickly. "I don't have time to be lonely."

"It takes no time at all to be lonely," Brian remarked. His face reddened, and he grabbed his wine glass to take a long sip. His gaze shifted to the painting on the wall.

"Why did you pick a spot so remote? Why on your uncle's property?" She pressed.

"Well, it was free for starters." I faked a laugh and sipped my wine, feeling the dreaded fingers of panic beginning to crawl along my spine. Aubrey knew I hated to talk about my feelings.

On my fifteenth birthday, she gave me a journal. It had one of the most beautiful covers I had ever seen. The cover was a deep mossy green, iridescent in the right light. Three golden elephants were engraved on the front. Two adult elephants and a baby. The largest one stood in the front of the line while the other two joined trunks and tails.

Tiny vines were engraved around the edges, and if you ran your fingers lightly over the cover, the pattern was smooth and soothing. For several weeks I felt like I would be somehow ruining the beauty by cracking it open and filling it with my teen angst. But Aubrey was relentless. She kept bugging me about the importance of expressing myself and writing about my crappy childhood. Once I started, it became another sort of obsession. I'd since filled nearly a dozen journals, but my favorite one will always be that green journal from Aubrey.

"I think maybe she's had too much to drink," I heard Brian whisper. Snapping out of my memory, my brain scrambled to recall what question I had left unanswered.

I shrugged. Do I get lonely? Yeah. But I felt lonely even in a crowd of people. Loneliness had been my bedfellow for so long, it was as if I'd reabsorbed a twin in utero. A wisp of a girl whose cells carried fear and pain instead of life and hope. Yet part of me relished the solitude. I like looking around my tiny space and knowing every inch of it belongs to me.

I could see sadness in Aubrey's gaze. "And your uncle? Is he a part of your life now?"

Despite my stoicism, Aubrey knew this was a core wound of mine. My only remaining family members had little to do with me. I grew up not only in the shadow of their happy family but also with the knowledge that I wasn't even a blip on their radar. Even now, this cut deep. My only glimpse into their lives was through social media. I would find out my cousins were in town and staying with my uncle, but they never reached out to me. I wasn't even an afterthought. It was as if I wasn't even a member of their family, just a smudged thumbprint on a forgotten mug in the back of a cupboard.

"No. Not really. I mean, he does allow me to plug into his electricity, and I leave him cash on his front step to pay for it every few months."

"Geez Willow. That sucks." Brian was quiet, but when he spoke up, his candor was refreshing.

"I'm sorry," Aubrey agreed. "I know you've always wanted a relationship with them. It's their loss."

I could feel the pinprick of heat behind my eyes as I swallowed the last of my wine down with a gulp. "It is what it is."

"Well, it sucks—is what it *is*. You would think that your uncle and his family would *want* you in their lives. Not ostracize you."

I shrugged. No matter how much it hurt me, the fact of the matter was they didn't care about me. There was little I could do to change their minds.

"Fuck 'em," Brian said as he took another swing of beer.

Aubrey laughed. "Tell us how you really feel, Bri."

"Anyway, thank you guys for having me and Zoe. Especially during this whole Covid thing. Do you need me to leave by a certain day? I don't want to overstay my welcome."

Aubrey stood and began ravaging the nearby candy dish. "You just got here. And you're already thinking of leaving?" she smirked.

I let the subject drop and resisted the urge to grab a piece of the unwrapped candy.

****

The rest of the evening was a relaxing haze. Zoe slept uninterrupted as we lounged in the living room and finished off the beer and wine. By the time I was ready for bed, my eyes were blurry with exhaustion. My breasts were aching with milk I hadn't drained. My body hummed with the warmth of the wine as I sank into the foreign mattress and began to dream...

I wandered through the halls of my old church school. Damp basement scents filled my nostrils and clung to my clothes as the mildewed brick and threadbare carpet brought me back to my childhood.

The hallway was empty and dimly lit. Each classroom doorway stood open as I slowly walked past each room. I stopped at the very end of the corridor. My feet froze in place as I looked up at the closed principal's door.

My gaze caught my reflection in the narrow window of the metal door. I could barely see myself there but recognized the woeful child standing before me. Smoothing my ankle-length, mint green skirt, I glanced down to fluff the bright, white lace edge as it grazed the floor. My scuffed, chocolate brown Mary Janes, passed down from some generous spirit who'd given the Calkins garbage bags full of used clothes and shoes for all of us this year. My hand reached up to turn the knob, and I studied my fingers for a moment.

They were the hands of a young girl: smooth and supple. Unmarked by the roughness of life, no knobby knuckles or puffy veins. I pushed the door open and held my breath as I stepped inside.

A cheap, gold-plated nameplate sat on Principal Pearce's desk. A familiar sense of dread and shame washed over me as I now stood in the center of the small room. There was barely enough space for the metal desk, chair, and row of filing cabinets. I knew exactly what I was looking for. I stopped in front of the last row of filing cabinets, pulling the tight drawer open as its cheap metal objected. The paddle sat on top of an old leather Bible. Its flat surface was the color of pea soup, worn from the countless spankings of guilt-ridden sinners.

Suddenly, my dream transported me further back to that sunny June day in fourth grade….

Aubrey and I gleefully followed our class out to the church parking lot. Each of us held a lilac-colored helium balloon. Our instructions had been to choose a scripture from the Bible that could change someone's life. There were only a few days left before summer vacation, and we were all relishing those final days where your day vacillated between busy work, cleaning out your desks and playing outside. Today, our entire school—all sixty-four of us—was going outside to release balloons to the world. We'd been given small strips of paper and purple ribbon to attach our message. After being lectured on the moral responsibility we each had to save the souls of as many people as possible, we wrote down our messages and headed outdoors.

I'd pulled out my Bible, flipping through to find an appropriate scripture to share with some lost soul. Aubrey sat nearby doing the same, a smug grin on her face. I knew exactly what she was planning, and I was in awe of her bravery. She'd slipped me a note when Mrs. Shelby wasn't looking.

Save your soul, leave the church, it said.

I looked at her quizzically as she shrugged her shoulders.

"That's your message?" I mouthed.

Aubrey nodded, watching Mrs. Shelby out of the corner of her eye. The teacher was busy unplugging the massive computer to wheel it down to the second graders.

"It's a better message than anything I'd write down

from the Bible." she whispered. "What are you gonna write?"

"I dunno, maybe something nice from Psalms?"

She giggled and shook her head. "Why not write lyrics to a Madonna song? It would be more interesting."

Aubrey knew I wasn't allowed to listen to Madonna, and wouldn't even know any of her songs. She also knew my overly guilty conscience wouldn't let me stray too far from the directions given.

"Do it," she said a bit louder than necessary.

I stared at my piece of paper, lost for a moment in a moral quandary. The wheels on the computer cart squealed along the hallway.

"Here, give it to me." Aubrey reached out her hand to take my paper.

I handed it to her, swallowing down the guilt of what I was allowing her to do. She studied the blank form for a few seconds before putting something down and handing it back to me.

"A person's a person, no matter how small. -Dr. Suess."

I smiled. Aubrey was a huge Dr. Suess fan, and made no secret of the fact that she thought his books contained more wisdom than most of the stuff we were forced to read. But what if the teacher asked to read what we wrote before we let our balloons go? Would I get into trouble? If God was always watching, as they said, would I be "sinning" by not following directions?

"All right class, tie your messages to your balloons and line up by the door." The teacher's voice interrupted my internal struggle. Aubrey grinned at me as I did what I was told and followed her to the door.

We walked down the hallway, and up the basement steps into the bright sunlight. The kids and teachers lined up in the parking lot, sweating and murmuring while we waited for Pastor Mettin to make an appearance. As the door to his private chambers swung open, I could feel my stomach tighten. Something about him made me dread his looming presence. We watched as he circled around us and took a stance in the middle of the parking lot. His booming voice filled the air.

"Students. Let us pray."

We bowed our heads obediently.

"Dear Heavenly Father. We thank you for this opportunity to share your Word. To share your message of redemption and love. You have guided us in selecting a message, and we know whoever reads this message will be touched by your grace. May this be a constant reminder that you are always watching over us and giving us opportunities to spread your holy word. And as we look up to the heavens, may we be reminded of our heavenly home and all the souls that we are responsible for saving so they may join us on those streets of gold in our final resting place, where we shall bask in your glory and worship you for all of our days. In the holy name of Jesus Christ, we ask this. Amen."

We raised our heads and lifted our balloons into the sky. I hoped mine would find a small, sad girl like me. One needing to be reminded that she counted. The only problem was the wind. A slight puff of air from the east grabbed my balloon at the exact wrong time and pulled it toward the large oak past the swing set.

Rather than heading to the playground with the rest of the kids, Aubrey and I made our way over to the massive tree at the edge of the parking lot.

"Oh, no!" I stood by the trunk looking up at the purple latex now lodged in a branch way beyond my reach. "Aub! What if they find out I didn't write a scripture?"

"You worry too much." She clucked her tongue at me. "No one's gonna read it anyway. Even IF our balloons reach someone, the pollution alone is gonna wear away our message." Aubrey had recently done a project for the science fair on pollution, and was convinced we were all slowly killing the earth in every way imaginable.

"Come on." She said,

I followed her to the other side of the tree so we could get a closer look at my balloon. "Look, if we both hang on that branch," she pointed to the closest one above our heads. "Our weight will pull it down slightly, and hit the branch above and loosen your balloon."

"Really?" I often doubted her logic, but always followed her instructions anyway. "Okay."

She counted us down from three, and we jumped to reach the middle branch above our heads. It looked small, but sturdy. My twiggy arms began to burn after a few seconds, and I could see Aubrey was also struggling to hold on. Before we could let go, the entire branch cracked and crashed down to the ground, bringing us with it. We sat on the lumpy grass, a bit stunned at the turn of events. Mrs. Reeta came running over.

"Oh my goodness, girls! What happened? Are you okay?" She crouched down to our level to check us for injuries.

I immediately began crying. Not because of any injury, but because I knew this would surely mean a trip to the principal's office.

"Willow, are you hurt?" she asked.

I shook my head and scrambled to my feet. Aubrey was already erect. Her eyes were downcast.

"Let's get you inside, shall we?"

"We're okay. Mrs. R. Can we just go play?" Aubrey smoothed her dress and looked longingly at the playground.

Mrs. Reeta looked at the broken branch now laying at our feet.

"I'm afraid we will have to figure out how to deal with this branch."

"Are we in trouble?" Dread began to fill my stomach.

"I'm sure it was an accident. But we'd better check in with Principal Pearce about how to handle this." Mrs. Reeta was my favorite teacher. Her soft lilting voice was soothing, and her use of affirming stickers always made me happy. Yet as a woman in the church, she never seemed to question Principal Pearce's stern methods of punishment. Somehow, I felt this had more to do with his maleness than his role. I'd overheard her complaining to the first-grade teacher about his roughness with the students the other day. For a brief moment, I'd felt hopeful she would stand up to him. Then she pointed out that since God placed men in a position of power over women, he must know best what God wanted.

I swallowed down the remainder of my disappointment in her as she pulled out her walkie-talkie.

"Principal Pearce, we have a bit of a situation here with a broken tree branch. No one is hurt. But I'm sending Aubrey and Willow in to see you. Is that okay?"

A staticky confirmation sank our hearts as she sent us back up to the building.

Stepping out from the brightness of the day into the cool, dim interior, everything became temporarily black as my eyes adjusted.

"Just great," Aubrey huffed as I followed her down the stairs, "Stupid P brain is probably gonna spank us."

Pinpricks of tears gathered behind my eyes as I swallowed down a lump of terror. "Do you really think we'll get spanked?" She shrugged, glancing back at me. "I'm sorry. I thought the branch was strong enough to hold us. I didn't mean to break it." I muttered toward my ill-fitting shoes.

Aubrey stopped mid-step and turned to face me.

"Do not for one minute think this is your fault, Willow. The only thing to be sorry for is that we are stuck going to this stupid school with these power-hungry morons." She stared at me until I gave her a half-hearted grin. "Are you scared?"

I nodded.

"Me too. Let's get this over with." She pulled the door open, and I followed her around the corner to the tiny office.

"Girls." Principle Pearce cleared his throat and stood as we entered his office. "Are you okay?" We nodded, both remaining silent. "Please sit down. Let's chat for a moment."

We settled into the hard chairs on the other side of his desk. I wished I could scooch my chair closer to Aubrey's.

"What happened?"

"Well, you see, Sir," Aubrey began, "My balloon got stuck in the tree branch, and we thought we could hang on one of the lower branches and knock it loose."

"Hmm. Did it knock it loose?"

We shook our heads.

"And is that how the branch broke? From hanging on it?"

"Yes, but it was purely accidental." Aubrey jutted out her lower lip a bit. "We never intended to break it."

Just last week Pastor Mettin had led a chapel service where he spoke about intent. I hoped Aubrey's message wasn't lost on him.

"Umm hmm. I understand. Yet, you did manage to damage school property. Willow, why didn't you just tell the teacher the balloon got stuck before hanging on the branch?"

My voice froze in my throat, and I shrugged at him mutely. Although his tone was kind, something about him unnerved me.

"It's my fault, sir. I wasn't thinking. I just grabbed Willow's hand and pulled her toward the tree. I thought the branch would snap up and knock the balloon loose, and we wouldn't have to bother anyone. Are you gonna spank us?"

Aubrey seemed full of courage to me. I still couldn't even manage to speak.

"As you know, your parents, or guardians, have both signed forms to allow us to discipline as we see fit. Proverbs chapter 23, verses 13 and 14: 'Withhold not correction from the child: for if thou beatest him with the rod, he shall not die. Thou shalt beat him with the rod, and shalt deliver his soul from hell.'"

"So that's a yes," Aubrey whispered.

"Unfortunately, there is still the matter of destroying school property. Even though you did not intend to break anything, a large branch has been broken off of one of God's creations. Mr. Stevens is heading outside soon to clean up the branch. In the meantime, we need to set an example for the other children about the importance of taking care of God's earth and school property."

"But it was an accident!" Aubrey interrupted.

He ignored her and continued speaking. "You will each be spanked seven times, as a reminder of God's perfection and our earthly desire to reach that perfection." He stood and walked over to the top drawer of the last filing cabinet and pulled out the ping pong paddle. "Willow, please step out of the office for a moment. You may wait in the hallway."

I tried to catch Aubrey's gaze before I left, but she sat stoically, staring out the small basement window. As I closed the door behind me, I took a few steps away from the office and leaned back against the cool painted brick wall. Above the din of my classmates outdoors, I could clearly hear seven slow, satisfying smacks bringing her closer to God.

Chapter Thirteen

April 24, 2021

Sunshine squeezed its way through the crack in the pulled curtains and attacked my left eye. I blinked and held my hand up against the offending brightness. Zoe stirred in the playpen beside me but remained asleep.

If I was quiet enough, I might be able to take a quick shower before she awoke. She was a solid sleeper, and even if she woke up, she would occupy herself for a few minutes with the toys scattered around her. Slinking out of bed, I mentally reviewed my outfit options. Rather than try to silently dig through my things, I brought the whole bag with me to the bathroom. Compared to the hole in the wall that housed my tiny lavatory, Aubrey's space was enormous.

Yesterday's incident with Zoe's blow-out didn't afford me much time to appreciate the spectacular shower and vanity. Not only did she have a full-sized tub, she had two sinks! Each of the raised copper bowls had its own scented soap and separate drawers underneath. I snickered at the concept of his and her washing areas but admired it anyway. A soak in the huge tub would feel luxurious, but I didn't have time. I opted for a quick shower and skipped the dreaded shaving, as I would be covered in my jeans and sweater.

By the time I got back to my room, Zoe was

awake. She was sitting in the middle of a lump of toys and chattering happily.

"Da!" She exclaimed, raising her arms to me.

Da? My eyes filled with hot emotion. Did she mean "Dad"? Since there was no dad in her life, I doubted that's what she was trying to say. *Dog*, perhaps? I scooped her up and held her close.

"Ma!" This word melted my heart as she smiled at me before assaulting my nose with the reality of her putrid diaper. I quickly changed her, and we made our way downstairs. My phone buzzed from my jeans pocket.

"Good morning." Aubrey set a platter of pancakes on the table.

"Good morning. You didn't have to cook for me." I pulled my phone out and glanced at the screen.

—How did you sleep? Did you have any interesting dreams you wrote down for your editor? Keep turning your pain into art, babe. Isn't that what your therapist said? Minus the babe part, I hope. LOL.—

I felt my cheeks redden at the use of the word *babe*, and quickly slid my phone back into my pocket.

"Don't worry, it's not gonna happen often. Can Zoe eat pancakes yet?" Aubrey's back was to us as she stacked a plate full of fluffy goodness.

"She can hold onto one. Thanks." I said as I leaned down to smell the luxurious scent of her baby shampoo.

Aubrey grabbed the orange juice from the fridge and set it down on the table. Zoe was perched on my lap, trying to grab any object within her reach, so I started pushing everything further away from her potential grasp. I ripped a pancake in half and once it was cool enough I handed it to Zoe, which she immediately started to gum.

"How did you sleep?" Aubrey asked while sitting down.

"Pretty good. I had some vivid dreams, though. Remember the tree branch we broke when we were little?"

"Oh my gosh! I forgot all about that! It was the only time I was ever spanked." She laughed.

I bristled, wishing I could have said the same.

"What do you want to do today? I have no work for the next three days, not that we can really go anywhere with Covid and all." Aubrey poured a generous amount of maple syrup over her pancakes.

"Um, I dunno. I just thought we could hang here. Zoe and I can head home anytime you want though. I don't want to overstay our welcome."

"You just got here! I haven't seen you in forever, and who knows how long this whole lockdown thing is gonna last. Don't talk about leaving just yet. I'm afraid Brian has to work today, so he won't be back till dinner. So, it's just us girls."

"He left for work already?"

"He's upstairs in the attic. We created our workspaces up there. He's working from home today but does go into the office a few times a week.

"That's cool," I lied. I liked Brian. But knowing he was home, even if it was on the third floor, somehow took away from *girl* time. Brian had always been nice to me, but I wouldn't necessarily consider him a friend. Men always seemed to regard me as, well—to actually *not* regard me at all. When I was in their presence, it was as if I didn't exist. Perhaps I exuded a *do not acknowledge me* vibe. I'd rarely dated, preferring occasional dates to full blown relationships. An unwanted flash of my baby boy popped into my mind, the ripping pains that pushed him from my body. His lifeless form I bundled and later buried. I pushed the thought away and kissed Zoe's sweet head. She was mine. Conceived in that last fumbling liaison. This was my new truth.

"Earth to Willow." I heard Aubrey snicker and brought myself back to the present.

"So, what do you want to do today?" She repeated.

"Oh, um, well, Zoe will nap this afternoon, so I'm not sure. Maybe go for a walk? We are pretty self-sufficient. Is there something I can help out with, like dinner?"

"I thought we would just order a pizza tonight if that's okay," said Aubrey.

"Of course. I love pizza! Is there anything around the house you need help with? Like, any projects you've been putting off?" Unfurling Zoe's tiny hand, I pulled a soggy lump of pancake away, replacing it with a new piece before she could protest.

"Do you really think I'm going to put you to work during your visit?" She shook her head. "Any projects I might have been perfecting the art of procrastination on will still be around after you're gone. I'm not wasting my time with you by relining the cupboards or some nonsense like that. I just want to spend time catching up. It's been way too long. Honestly, I was kinda surprised you agreed to come. I figured you were too busy with Zoe and everything."

Her candor inspired me. Aubrey had always seemed to find it easy to speak her mind. I wished my brain would stop second-guessing every single thought that popped into my prefrontal cortex. What would it even be like to not constantly worry about what other people thought of me? Even the freedom of that concept exacerbated my anxiety. On the rare occasion I actually chose to share a thought; it had already been filtered through several sieves of self-judgment. It felt comfortably neurotic.

"How about a walk then?" Zoe had grown bored of the mush of food in front of her and was signing that she was finished with her meal.

"Oh. You're all done?" I signed to Zoe. "All done eating?" She repeated the gesture.

"Oh my God, she knows sign language?" Aubrey widened her eyes in surprise, and I felt a bit of pride at her acknowledgment.

"She just knows a few signs so far. I started teaching her about a month ago. So far, she knows, *done, up, milk,* and *more.*

"How cool! I remember reading about how babies can learn to sign before they speak. You're such a good mom."

Aubrey held my gaze until I allowed myself to smile at the compliment. She knew even though I'd always wanted a baby, I was also terrified that I would be a crappy mom.

"Thanks, Aub. I'm trying. I know I'm bound to muck it up somehow."

"Well, seeing as you've already been well versed in what *not* to do, I think you're a step ahead of most people.

"I hope so." I swallowed down my unspoken fears.

****

To: Melaniewalker@catharsistimepress.com
From:Willowmorgan666@gmail.com
Subject: Age 13
Mel, Here's another one. Are you sure you want such small snippets? -W

"Did you read your Bible this morning?" Mrs. Calkins handed me the off-brand cereal and the box of powdered milk.

"Yes, ma'am."

"Out loud?" She raised her eyebrows at me as if hoping to catch me in a lie.

"Um, well, Molly was still sleeping, so I just read to myself this morning."

"We've talked about this, Willow. It is important to read your Bible out loud. God wants to hear His words coming from your mouth."

I highly doubted God cared, but I nodded in agreement. It was always better to just agree with Mrs. Calkins, no matter how absurd it sounded.

"Next time, come downstairs so you can read aloud. It'll do you good to get out of your room anyway. Now go get Molly up for school. She should have been up by now. Soon, she will reach the age of accountability, and she'll have to make the choice of choosing the path of the righteous or damnation."

According to the Calkins, the age of accountability was twelve. At twelve, you were apparently old enough to take ownership of the status of your soul. You were responsible for your "sins." Making sure you did everything you could to remove any temptation of sin was of the utmost importance. Unfortunately, they also believed that most things were sinful. For example, not only was praying before eating mandatory, something as simple as putting a piece of gum in your mouth without thanking the Lord for it was sinful. Doing so was being ungrateful and not properly acknowledging God's blessings. The other day I'd been caught with a piece of candy in my mouth. Mr. Calkins had been secretly watching me from the other room as I unwrapped a Jolly Rancher. As its bold, tart-sweetness filled my mouth, he came storming into the room.

"Willow! Did you thank the Lord for that before consuming it?"

I stared at him, frozen, and unsure of what to do. He waited, his eyes boring into my guilt, until I shook my head to admit my short-sightedness.

"Spit it out." He demanded, his palm upturned beneath my chin.

Of course, I did as I was told. After which I was sent to my room with no dinner for the night. Thankfully, I had a hidden stash of Jolly Ranchers tucked away in the back of my closet. Just to be safe from an afterlife of hellfire and brimstone, I mumbled a prayer before enjoying each and every one of them as my stomach rumbled in protest of my punishment.

Chapter Fourteen

We stared in silence at the television. Zoe was in bed for the night, and Aubrey, Brian, and I lounged in the living room with another bottle of wine. The death toll was climbing. Covid had seemed to take over the world, leaving death and destruction in its wake. The CDC now officially recommended wiping down all of your groceries before putting them away. That was assuming you were actually going into the stores instead of the safer alternative of online shopping. I'd already been wiping everything down and found it comforting to think other people would finally be doing the same. Earlier in the broadcast, they had interviewed a teenager who witnessed an elderly man being pushed aside so someone else could buy the last package of toilet paper. The man was now being treated for a broken hip.

"What the hell?" Aubrey poured herself another glass of Chardonnay. I was still nursing mine, and Brian was working on his second beer. "Have people always been this cruel?"

"Yes," said Brian. "They were just better at hiding it."

"I dunno," Aubrey countered. "I still think people are basically good at heart. They are just afraid. They're acting out of fear."

"That's a cop-out. They might be afraid, or

anxious, or stressed, or whatever. But it doesn't give people the right to be assholes."

"Exactly!" I had been zoning out of the conversation, so when I brought my attention back and chimed in, it came out a bit louder than I'd anticipated. A familiar heat crept into my cheeks as I reached for the bottle of wine. My anxiety prompted me to top off my glass.

"I agree with you, Brian. People are generally assholes, and they are only looking out for themselves. So what if that guy ran out of toilet paper? Even if he had to use his own sock to wipe his butt, it doesn't give him the right to push over an old guy. I hope they prosecute him."

"I heard he tried to leave the store before getting caught, but some little girl grabbed onto his leg and yelled for help before he could escape!" Aubrey stretched her leg over Brian's, and he immediately began to rub her feet.

"Seriously? Is that true? Where did you hear that? Man, if it's true, she deserves an award or something. That's pretty brave," Brian chuckled.

"I think I read it on online or something." Aubrey shrugged.

"Well, *there's* a reliable source." I laughed. "I have a love-hate relationship with social media. I'm nosey and I want to see what people are up to, but then I see all the cool things they post about and how fit they are, or vacations they go on, and I just end up feeling bad about myself."

Aubrey and Brian nodded.

"I think social media is Satan's lair." Brian scoffed. "Look at all the political divide. I've unfriended like half of my friends!"

"Are you one of those people who have like four hundred *friends*? I think I only have twenty-seven online friends." *Was this a reflection of how unpopular I was? Did I care?*

"Maybe not four hundred, maybe like two hundred and fifty? Honestly, I don't know. People just send me requests, and I accept them. But recently, people started posting really crazy stuff online. Like this dude I went to high school with who was posting lots of stuff about guns, his rights, and anti-liberal crap. I finally couldn't stand looking at his posts anymore, so I unfriended him. It was really stressing me out to see all the crap he was putting online."

"I told him I thought that was a cop-out," Aubrey spoke up. "Just unfriending someone like that? How is that actually gonna change anything? Why not have a dialogue? Find out why he believes what he believes. Learn from each other."

Brian narrowed his eyes and stopped rubbing Aubrey's feet. She responded with a sigh and tucked her legs underneath her.

"I don't have the energy for that. Besides, I'm not gonna change the guy's mind. He was an asshole back in school. I doubt he's gonna change."

I watched the exchange, noting the tension in the air. A bleak silence filled the room and was suddenly interrupted by Zoe's muffled cry from upstairs.

"That's my cue," I tried to sound upbeat. "Be right back." My body swayed slightly as I stood. Hopefully, they didn't notice the wine was catching up with me. By the time I carefully made my way up the plush stairs, Zoe was screaming. I bent to scoop her up, and she quieted immediately.

"What's wrong, baby girl? Did you have a bad dream?" Smoothing away the damp hair from her forehead, I noted how hot her skin was. She clung to me, her tiny fingers clasping at my shirt. "Are you sick?"

I flipped on the light by the bed, and she blinked at me in response. Her tiny face was mottled pink from crying, and her skin was clammy and warm. Too warm. Up until now, Zoe had never been sick. She'd been to the pediatrician several times since her birth and so far had been the picture of health. In fact, the first time that I brought her in after she'd arrived at my doorstep, I thought for sure someone would somehow know she wasn't really mine. No one questioned it. It was almost too easy.

My labor had started early and was lightning fast. That first jolt of pain had ripped through me midway through watching an old sappy-sweet family show. By the time the main character had her weekly epiphany, my son had violently entered and then slipped from this world. Exhausted, ashamed, and spent, I held him until my bleeding slowed. I cradled him as his tiny body grew cold and stiff. I swaddled his silent form and buried him deep underneath my rose bushes out back. Dirt caked and swollen, I collapsed on the couch and woke up seventeen hours later. Those handful of days were a drugged-like blur until I'd opened my door to find Zoe on my front step.

No one had questioned that she was mine. In the midst of an invisible apocalypse, everything had fallen into place. Her birth certificate, health insurance, all of it had been done electronically. Sure, I'd brought her into an actual office for her weights and shots, but no one ever questioned it. She was mine.

And now she was sick. *What if it's this Covid thing? What if the devious, cruel God I'd grown to hate was hating me back?*

"Is she okay?" Aubrey was leaning against the bedroom door frame.

"I think she has a fever. Do you have a thermometer?"

She disappeared down the hallway, returning with a small electronic device. I stared at it for a moment, trying to make sense of where it went.

"Just hold it up to her forehead." Aubrey moved closer to us.

Zoe whimpered in my arms as I took her over to the bed, holding her on my lap. The device beeped as I held it near her skin.

"One hundred degrees. That's a fever. Shoot. I don't even know where the nearest pediatrician is. I don't even have baby medicine with me or anything. What was I thinking?"

Aubrey began to pace around the room.

"What if it's Covid?" I spoke my fear out loud.

"Don't think that. It's not. It's just a mild fever. What about her pediatrician back home? Can you call them?"

"I guess I could call the after-hours number. Good idea." I scooted closer to the bedside table and grabbed my phone, scrolling through the numbers with one hand. My heart raced as I dialed the number and explained Zoe's symptoms to the on-call operator. Zoe had fallen back asleep. A tiny furnace braced against my chest. The call was abrupt, and I was told a doctor would call right back.

"What's going on?" Brian peeked his head into the room. Aubrey and I stared at the phone, willing it to ring. A few minutes later it did, and after a short conversation with her doctor, I hung up feeling slightly less catastrophic. Since her fever wasn't super high, she didn't have a cough, trouble breathing, or any other symptoms the only course of action for tonight was to give her some medicine and wait for her fever to subside. Without even being asked, Brian offered to run to the overnight pharmacy to grab some over the counter fever-reducing medicine. I tucked Zoe into the bed beside me and studied her eyelashes as she dozed.

While I waited for Brian to return, I scrolled through my phone in a vain attempt to distract myself. I clicked on the newest unread text that I somehow missed earlier. —*Do you miss me?*—

I studied the words, already knowing my answer, but not wanting to admit it. Sighing, I tapped on another icon to scroll through social media. My eyes blurred as I mindlessly sifted through the posts. Brian returned in record time.

Sneaking liquid medicine into a baby's mouth is surprisingly easy. Zoe slumbered on, swallowing the sweet syrup with a drowsy gulp. Aubrey had climbed onto the other side of the bed; Zoe was asleep between us. Her cheeks were still flushed with fever, and other than an occasional murmur, she was quiet.

****

Hours later, a sliver of sunlight through the curtain woke me. I turned to look at Zoe, who slumbered on. The medicine seemed to have worked. Her skin was cooler, and she seemed comfortable. Aubrey's back was to us, and her breathing was even and slow. I assumed she was still asleep. I shifted my weight to carefully sit at the edge of the bed and lined up a bunch of pillows along Zoe's side. Then I threw the largest pillow to the floor for good measure. If she somehow managed to roll past my pillow guards, perhaps another one on the floor would cushion her fall.

My bladder beckoned me to trust she'd be safe as I made my way to the bathroom. I rushed my trip to the toilet, splashing cold water on my face after scrubbing my hands twice with the apple-scented soap. I reached for the hand towel but paused as I turned the tap back on and washed a third time. Knowing it made no sense didn't stop me from feeling better on some level.

By the time I returned to the bedroom, Aubrey was awake. She sat leaning against the bed frame, scrolling through her phone.

"Hey," she whispered, looking up.

"Hey, I didn't mean for you to have to sleep in here with us."

"Huh? Oh, I just totally crashed. Must have been the wine. Where's Brian?"

I shrugged as she returned her gaze to her phone. Zoe stirred, and I instinctively held my breath. Her tiny fists rose and rubbed at her eyes as she blinked them open. Her bright blue gaze searched my face as she greeted me with a knowing smile. She held her hand out to me, clasping her fingers into a fist and slowly tapping her fingertips toward her palm. *Milk.* She was hungry.

"What's that mean?" Aubrey eased her way off the bed and smoothed the blanket.

"She wants milk. Guess she's feeling better."

Feeling grateful she seemed fever free and happy, I scooped her up.

"Do you know how to make a bottle of formula?"

"You're hilarious," Aubrey said. "Nope. I don't. But I have a feeling I'm gonna learn. I'd rather be on milk duty than diaper duty, though. What should I do?"

"I left the can on the counter by your stove. The directions are on the back. I think I left a few sterilized bottles next to it. Do you mind?" I lay Zoe on the plush carpet to change her diaper.

"I'll give it a try. Lemme just check to see if Brian is awake yet. Meet ya downstairs?"

"Thanks," I nodded.

To: Melaniewalker@catharsistimepress.com
From:Willowmorgan666@gmail.com
Subject: Age 14

Mel, I'm so sorry to hear your mom has Covid! Is she okay so far? Is she able to stay home and recover? Obviously, there's no rush in getting back to me. I'll just keep sending you snippets as they come to me. Sending you and your family positive vibes. -W

Feeding the babies in the church nursery was one of my favorite things. Past the large room with rows of stacked cribs attached to the far wall was another door. Secretly, I thought of the door as a magical portal to another universe. Although, there were no fur coats leading to a wintery wonderland. Beyond the plain dark wood was a small empty corridor.

The tiny hallway wove its way into a deeper, hidden room. The walls were bare but padded with soundproofing. Two wooden rocking chairs with worn cushions faced each other in silence. The plush blue carpet was dark, reminiscent of a pond at twilight. My socked feet sank into the softness as I carried baby Millie to the nearest chair. Her mother had hurriedly handed her off to me at the nursery door.

"I just made her a bottle before leaving home. It's still warm. I'm late for praise and worship. Could you feed her and put her down for a nap?" Mrs. Sparke pushed Millie into my arms as she bent to set the diaper bag near my feet.

"Thanks!" She disappeared before Millie could begin to protest.

I loved Millie. But then again, I loved them all. Who wouldn't adore those cherubic faces who looked to me for comfort? It was as if I possessed a miraculous power over even the fussiest of babies. Millie often cried for other nursery staff, recently causing one of the tweens to sneak out into the congregation during service to search for her mother. But she never cried when I was with her.

We made our way to the rocker, and I settled her on my lap with her bottle. The wall facing the sanctuary was covered with thick blue curtains. Today the curtains were closed, and the ceiling speaker that often hosted our pastor's shouted sermons was turned off.

One Sunday, before any children or nursery staff arrived, I'd worked up the courage to open the mysterious door and explore the sacred space. I'd peeked behind the curtain and was surprised to see a row of dark windows that allowed one to see into the back of the large sanctuary. It was as if no one could see me, though. Was this a one-way mirror? And if so, why?

A few of the faithful were already sitting in pews, some praying. One tall man Aubrey and I nicknamed

Scarecrow was dancing in the aisle, praying loudly in tongues. His liquid movements interspersed with jaunty twitches of his limbs. He did that all the time. In fact, an elder of the church was usually stationed nearby. I was never quite sure why, though. Even on the days when he shouted or sang nonsensical gibberish into the air, no one stopped him. The protective barrier of the dark glass was a bit hard to see through. My own reflection appeared more distorted than usual.

Sitting now in the silence was comforting, and I found myself getting drowsy as the warm Millie bundle snuggled against my flat chest. Her bottle began to slip from her grip, rousing me from my near slumber. Something about the room was both unnerving and comforting. If I ignored the small dome with the blinking red light on the ceiling and the mysterious windows behind the blue curtains, I could pretend I was in my own fantasy realm. A soft, sweet home with no space for evil witches or creepy half-man beasts.

My mind wandered as I imagined what this magical place would look like. A beautiful never-winter garden full of vibrant, colorful flowers and butterflies. I would relish walking through this sanctuary. The grass was velvet beneath my bare feet. I would walk and walk until I reached the clearing. And there *she* would be waiting for me. My beautiful mother. Her arms stretched out to greet me and gather me in for a hug. She would be tall and beautiful, with flowing dark hair. Her body soft and warm, and in her embrace there was no reminder of death or absence. It felt like what I imagined bliss to be.

"Willow?" Mrs. Stevens whispered from around the bend in the hallway.

I blinked my eyes open, swiping away a random tear that insisted on residing.

"Are you okay?" She moved gingerly, sitting across from me in the other rocker. "Are you crying?"

"No." I'm sorry. I think I fell asleep. I'm sorry, I didn't mean to." Was I going to get in trouble? What if I wasn't allowed to work in the nursery anymore? That would mean I would have to go back to attending the two to three-hour Sunday service. I should never have fallen asleep!

"Sleeping babies have that effect on people." She chuckled quietly. "Don't worry. I just wanted to make sure you were both okay. You've been back here for a while."

I shifted in the chair, beginning to lift Millie and stand. Mrs. Stevens motioned for me to sit back down. "Why don't you just stay here and rest with her for a bit? It's so peaceful back here. There are only three kids out front, and I have two junior helpers, so we are more than covered. She gently placed her hand on my shoulder as she stood.

"If you ever need anything, Willow, I'm here for you. You know that, right?" I smiled at her and nodded. Hoping my face would not betray the pinprick of warmth I felt in my chest at her kindness. It was an unfamiliar and uncomfortable sensation as if I'd been cracked open and left on display for the world to see my innards.

Chapter Fifteen

May 2, 2021

Had we overstayed our welcome? Zoe and I had been here now for nearly two weeks. Our routine was becoming too comfortable, and I worried Aubrey and Brian were being too polite to say anything to prompt us to leave. The Covid death toll kept rising. Stories of overcrowded hospitals and a lack of ventilators filled the news. Travel was strongly discouraged, and in some cases, borders were even closed. But I missed my tiny house. I missed the solitude. Yet the warmth of friendship kept me grounded here during a time full of unknowns.

"I think we may head home soon." I tried to sound casual over coffee this morning. Aubrey had already been upstairs working online for a few hours and had come down to the kitchen to replenish her mug. It had given me plenty of time to return Cody's texts without feeling like I was being rude. He'd been texting me daily since I'd left, and I finally gave in and allowed myself the pleasure of messaging him back regularly. Getting close to anyone had always been a challenge for me, but somehow texting felt a bit safer. I'd begun to share more of myself, and so far, I hadn't managed to scare him off.

"What? Why? Don't leave yet. We love having you

here!" Aubrey interrupted my train of thought.

"Besides, you and Zoe are the only people in our bubble right now. If you leave, it'll just be the two of us for who knows how long."

"Wouldn't you like that?" I'd always assumed Aubrey was enamored with Brian. Wasn't she?

"Well, I mean, yes. Um, sure." She paused. "But I like how things are right now." She gave me a look I couldn't quite decipher.

"It's been nice having the two of you here. You're an extension of our family. I've always kinda imagined wanting to pursue communal living," she said casually.

"*Communal?* What are you talking about?" I tried to catch her gaze as she backed out of the room. "Aubrey? What are you talking about?"

"I should have never said anything." She grabbed a bottle of water from the fridge. "I've gotta run back to this online meeting. Don't consider leaving yet, okay? Let's talk about this more later. I'll be breaking for lunch in like an hour. Okay?" She peeked her head back into the doorway and then disappeared before I could respond.

Communal living? What is she talking about? I'd never heard her mention anything remotely like that before. Maybe she was just joking? She must be joking. I pushed the mystery aside and turned my attention back to Zoe. She was sitting on the kitchen floor, playing with two large metal bowls and a wooden spoon I'd grabbed for her. I placed my hand on her silky hair and felt the warmth of her tiny head. *What if something happens to her?* Violent images began to fill my mind. I imagined a police officer suddenly pounding on the door, barging in, and taking her from me. Somehow, they knew she wasn't mine. Another unwanted image emerged. Zoe's tiny body lying in a huge hospital bed. Tubes everywhere. A looming ventilator taking up most of the room. Me, not allowed in to see her, to hold her. Me, alone, standing on her tiny grave. *Stop.* I reprimanded myself. *Stop.* Zoe's banging on the pot brought me back to reality. Standing up, I poured myself another steaming cup of caffeine. *Should we stay?*

****

To: Melaniewalker@catharsistimepress.com
From:Willowmorgan666@gmail.com
Subject: Age 10
Mel, Is your mom okay? How are you? I'm so worried. Should I even be sending you this? I don't want to be a bother. Thinking of you all. -W

"They could come for you in the middle of the night." Mr. Calkins' gravelly voice admonished me. "Be prepared. The book of Revelations warns us the end is nigh. We must be prepared." I was trapped in my room. He stood in our doorway, blocking us from leaving. Molly's tiny body trembled beside me on the bed. I grabbed her hand under the blanket, hoping if we remained silent, he would end his sermon early and leave us alone. He let us lay together for story time, but made Molly return to her bed when he was done. Usually after waiting for a few minutes, she would sneak back under the covers with me.

"They will come like a thief in the night," he continued. "Jesus warns us they will come. It is a test of our faith. Do you understand?" He stared at us until we both nodded. I had no idea what he was talking about. He'd initially come up to read to us and tuck us in, but often he decided to preach.

"I want to play you a song. Girls, you need to know this stuff. I'll be right back." He left the room as we pulled the blankets tighter up to our chins.

"What's he talking about?" Molly tried to keep her chin from quivering. "Who is coming for us? Are the doors locked? Are they coming tonight?"

"I don't know. Something he must have learned in church this week. Don't worry. It's all made up, Molly. He doesn't know what he's talking about. Don't let it scare you. We are safe." Even as I said it, part of me remained scared. I tried to reassure her and remind myself that most of what he said was delusional. But despite my efforts, I was terrified.

He returned with the portable record player and a record. On the cover was a large, glossy photo of a white man with a huge blonde afro. He wore a flannel shirt and dark wooden beads around his neck. Mr. Calkins bent to plug in the player, pushing the barbies on our dresser top aside to make room for the device. He slid the record out of its cover and gingerly placed it on the sphere. A mellow voice filled the air. Guitar accompanied the tenor. The melody would have been almost peaceful if it wasn't for the lyrics.

"Like a thief in the night they will come.
Ask if you're a child of the Son.
They will knock on your door and decree,
It's choose Him or it's choose me.
Deny Jesus Christ, or I'll take your life.
Die for Him, or live for me."

The lyrics were haunting and confusing. I tuned out the rest of the song. Imagining I was in in a land of make believe sitting in a cozy cottage by the fire. I was safe. In my imagination I saw myself snug and content in a wooden rocking chair. The fire crackled and popped as I felt its warmth fill the room.

"Willow? Did you hear what I said?" he sounded annoyed, his voice becoming louder. Molly squeezed my hand.

"Hmm?"

"What would you choose if they came to our door?" he waited for a response, but all I gave him was a shrug.

"The Bible tells us we will be tested. But only the righteous will have eternal life. So even if they come, even if they line us up and hold a gun to our heads asking us to deny Jesus Christ as our savior, we have to be prepared. We have to choose Christ. Even if they kill us, it's the only way we will be saved from an eternal damnation in hell. Burning in hell for all eternity. Is that what you want, girls?"

Molly and I stared at him in silence. Her petal pink lips agape.

"Well? What would you choose?"

"C-choose Jesus?" Molly whispered.

"That's right, baby! Choose Jesus! Always choose Jesus!" he beamed and bent to pull the plug from the wall. Scooping up the record player, he abruptly left the room. The album cover still lay on our dresser. We waited a beat to see if he would return. After listening to his footsteps retreat down the stairs, I popped out of bed and grabbed the glossy cardboard face. Tossing it on the floor beside the dresser, I slid it underneath with my foot. My pajama footies catching on the rough wooden floor. Once the afro'd man was no longer visible, I slid back under the covers with Molly.

"Do you think they will come for us tonight?" she repeated. I could see my own terror in her gaze.

"Shh." I wrapped my arm around her as she leaned against my shoulder. "Nothing like that is going to happen. It's all made up. No one is going to come here and do that to us. I won't let them." I pictured us all lined up in the kitchen, a man holding a gun to my foster father's head. *Shoot him,* I thought. *Shoot him, and then we will be safe.*

"Just forget the whole thing. He doesn't know what he is talking about."

"But I don't want to go to hell." Molly started sucking on the end of her braid. Whenever she began to feel really anxious, she always resorted to sucking on her hair.

"Shh." I pulled her closer. "There's no such thing as hell. And even if there was, you would never end up there."

It took a few minutes of stroking Molly's arm for her to begin to settle. Eventually, I felt her body relax, and her breathing become slow and steady. I stared at the ceiling, willing my eyes to become heavy with sleep. But sleep never came.

****

May 3, 2021

"Oh my God, Aub. George McMiller has Covid." Brian shoved open the kitchen door. The sweet scent of spring air seeped into the room as he bent to retrieve another bag of groceries from outside. We waited until he pulled all four bags inside, setting them on the floor beside the stove. While he washed his hands, Aubrey and I got to work wiping down each item with alcohol wipes.

"McMuscle? That's awful. He is the epitome of good health. Does he know how he got it? Do you have to get tested now?"

"Don said I have to get tested since I stopped by the office last week." Brian left the damp hand towel on the counter and pulled out a wipe. He grabbed the gallon of milk and wiped it down quickly. I tried to ignore the fact that his version of clean was different from my own, and I resisted the urge to wipe it down again. My hands burned with the desire to wash them again.

"But you only ran into the building for like five minutes just to drop off paperwork." Aubrey protested.

"I know, but anyone who set foot in the building in the last two weeks has to be tested. Don is being a stickler."

"Does that mean we have to be tested too?" I asked. The skin on my fingertips was peeling from all the daily hand sanitizer use and excessive washing. The pads of my fingers kept snagging on the cheap wipes. I tried doubling up the thin material, but it kept ripping as I wiped down the large bottle of laundry detergent. Was this necessary? Would it help prevent the spread, or were we all just fooling ourselves into a false sense of security? My whole life felt like one big delusion of safety.

A wave of guilt washed over me as I thought of all of the lives that Covid was stealing as I secretly enjoyed the overuse of sanitization. People around me were finally starting to think about germs the way I had been for my whole life. There was a form of comfort amidst the chaos. To me, the world was one big biosphere of putridity. It always had been, at least as long as I could remember. Each handshake, doorknob, credit card swipe filled my brain with images of microscopic invaders.

One of the appeals of my tiny house living was the amount of control I could have over my environment. Disinfecting was a breeze with such a small space. Cleaning took me less than thirty minutes, as long as I limited my hand washing between tasks. I was good at hiding the dysfunction of my brain, even here at Aubrey's. My brief bout of exposure therapy during high school after a particularly bad freak-out had taught me to keep my compulsive behaviors in check. I could usually limit myself to washing my hands like a regular person, but the *thought* of them not really being clean, that was another story. Now, in the midst of a pandemic, I had the freedom to allow myself to wipe, wash and sanitize until the voice in my head quieted, at least temporarily.

"Oh gosh, you're probably right. We probably all need to get tested now." Aubrey's voice rose in a slight panic. "I've heard the line of cars waiting for tests is hours long. We'll be there all day."

"I know. But at least we don't have to pay for them to stick Q-tips so far up our noses that they touch our brains." Brian scrunched up his nose at us and pulled out his phone. "I guess I should figure out where to go. I'll just get tested first. If I'm negative, then you guys don't have to bother getting tested."

"Can we do it that way? I thought we all would have to go." Aubrey was already scrolling through her phone.

"I'm not going unless I have to." They both looked up from their screens at me. "And what would they do about Zoe anyway? Babies can't get it, right? I mean, they aren't going to force me to test her too, will they?"

****

Zoe and I spent the morning puttering around the house. It was a beautiful spring day. The sun peeked out from behind the fluffy white clouds. We had no excuse not to take a walk. Pushing Zoe in the stroller was becoming a bit of a challenge. Her little personality was growing along with her. While strolling along the neighborhood, my gaze wandered up to the sky. I imagined breathing in the spaces of light between the branches of the trees.

My pulse slowed. Then, my serenity was interrupted as my foot squashed a small toy Zoe had thrown on the ground. I bent to pick it up as she giggled. Tucking in back in the stroller with her, I could see her little nose peeking out from between her jacket collar and the adorable bucket hat I'd ordered for her online. We continued on our walk until she threw the toy onto the ground again. This time I placed the toy in the bin beneath the stroller as she squealed in protest. Her unhappiness grew louder until I felt myself shrinking at the sound of her cries. Bending to return the toy to her chubby hand, she instantly quieted. She waited until I began pushing the stroller again and threw the item back onto the pavement with a laugh.

"You silly girl." I tried to keep my voice light but could feel the heat of irritation growing in my belly. "Let's go home." *Home*. It's what I wanted. My tiny home. My phone buzzed. It was time. Cody's texts were making me miss him more. We'd only hung out a few times before my trip here, but I had to admit I was looking forward to seeing him in person again.

****

Brian spiked a fever overnight. Exhausted and grumpy, he let Aubrey drive him to urgent care to get tested the next morning. Zoe and I waited. She lay on the fleece blanket I'd placed on the kitchen floor, playing with some stuffed animals that Aubrey had brought down from the attic, while I cleaned up the kitchen.

I opened up the music app on my phone and turned on the speaker so we could listen to my eighties playlist. Even though it was slightly before my time, I loved the music. Every time the song changed; I would take a peek at my screen to see who the artist was. Usually, I guessed correctly. After not being allowed to listen to "secular" music for most of my childhood, I was still catching up on decades of pop culture.

My phone buzzed. —*Whatcha doing now?*—

—*Listening to bad music, the kind that will send me to hell.*— I typed.

—*What? Like, Satanic music or something??*—

—*LOL. I think it's from the '80s. Does that count?*—

Chapter Sixteen

To: Melaniewalker@catharsistimepress.com
From:Willowmorgan666@gmail.com
Subject: Age 11
Mel, OMG I am so glad to hear your mom is doing
better! That's great news! What a relief! Has the rest of
your family stayed healthy? Brian is sick. I sure hope
it's not Covid. I'll probably be headed home soon.Stay
safe. -W

"What are you doing?" Mr. Calkins burst into the
room as Molly and I immediately stopped dancing. "Is
that Christian music?"

"It's Madonna!" Molly said gleefully. "She's the
mother of God!"

Mr. Calkins violently grabbed the cassette player
off our dresser, pulling the plug out of the wall as he
yanked.

Molly started to cry, and I placed a hand on her
arm to quiet her, hoping he would just take the music
and go. I was in no mood for a Biblical lecture.

"*This* Madonna," he paused for effect, "is *not* the
mother of God! How could you even say that? This
Madonna is evil! The devil is using her to corrupt our
youth. To make them think pre-marital sex is *not* an
abomination to our Lord! Like a thief in the night, she
is turning our children into sinners!" He boomed. He
softened after pausing his rant to notice Molly's tears.

Sitting on the edge of the bed, he motioned for us to join him, but we stayed put.

"Everything we do, everything"—he stared at us intently—"is meant to glorify God. He is a selfish God and is in need of our adoration! Every song we sing should be for His glory. His adoration!" He looked down at the bright pink double-deck cassette player in his hands. Molly and I had pooled our birthday money to buy it, along with two tapes. I waited to see if he would destroy it. Luckily, I had thought to keep my Debbie Gibson cassette in my pajama drawer. Shopping at thrift stores had its perks. Everything that was popular years ago was now discarded and cheap.

"God has given us the gift of song. It should be used to worship him. No more secular music, girls. It is of the devil. Do you understand?" Molly nodded obediently while I remained stoic.

"Come, girls," he said, removing the tape from the deck and setting our beloved device on my bedspread. "We have work to do."

We followed him through the dreary hall, down the dimly lit staircase, and out to the driveway. He handed the rectangle of plastic back to me. "Put it on the driveway." He commanded.

"What?"

"You heard me. Put it on the driveway. It needs to be destroyed. We are sending a message to the devil."

I thought of how excited Molly had been when we picked out the tape. She was still wearing one lace glove on her left hand. One of the bags of donated clothing we'd had gotten a few weeks ago had some homely doilies in it. When Mrs. Calkins half-heartedly gave us the bag of treasures, we had gleefully taken it to our room and dumped the contents onto our floor to investigate the treasures. Getting a bag of hand-me-downs was one of the most exciting treats for us. When the pieces of stained lace fell out, we looked at each other and immediately made plans for how to turn them into gloves. So far, the glove had gone unnoticed by Mr. C.

I did what he said and regretfully placed it on the driveway as he climbed into the station wagon.

"Stay out of the way!" He said cheerfully as he backed over our tiny link to the outside world. We watched him pull the car up and down the crumbling driveway a few times before putting the car in park and turning off the ignition. Molly's eyes were wide with surprise and sadness. I only felt anger, a burning hot sensation in my belly. It was a feeling that was becoming too familiar to me. Mr. C got out of the car and headed back to the house.

"Clean up this mess, girls. And then go get dressed for church."

He went inside, not seeming to care that he had damaged much more than the tape.

****

"It's positive," Aubrey announced as they walked through the door. Brian's eyes were glassy with fever, and I watched as she led him up the stairs. *So much for going home. I can't just up and leave Aubrey now. Now what? What if I get sick? What about Zoe?* My mind raced as it scrolled through all the worst-case scenarios. I rose to wash my hands, wincing a bit as the lather licked my cracked skin. A few minutes later, Aubrey tiptoed back down the stairs, joining me in the living room. Zoe had gone down for her nap already, and I was enjoying a mug of hot chocolate. Leaning forward, I grabbed the other steaming mug from the coffee table and handed it to her. She inhaled the rich cocoa aroma and took a sip.

"I can't believe it. He was so careful. I don't know what to do." She looked at me from over the edge of her mug.

"Do you have it too?" I tried to resist the urge to scoot further away from her on the couch. Even though, on some level, I knew we probably already all had it, I wanted to escape her germs.

"They made me get a test. It was negative. Isn't that strange? You'll have to get tested too now. I mean, my rapid test was negative. His was positive. We still have to wait a few days for the results of the other tests to know for sure."

"So, you could be positive?" I could feel my heart racing.

"Yeah, I guess. They told me that you should come in today and get tested, and in the meantime assume we all have it and we should isolate ourselves from each other."

"How do you isolate when we are all living in the same space?"

"I know, right? I mean, I guess I'll keep Brian in the bedroom, away from you and Zoe. Hopefully, the rest of us will stay healthy." She sighed.

"How do you feel?" I asked. "Do you feel sick?"

"I feel fine. Tired, I guess. But Brian was tossing and turning a lot last night, so I didn't sleep well."

"Since Zoe and I are in the spare room, where will you sleep?" *We should have never come to visit. If we had stayed home, we would have been safer.* My thoughts whirled around me, settling over my body like a shadowy weight.

"I'll be okay sleeping on the couch. Don't worry about it."

"Maybe Zoe and I should go home today. Then, we aren't in the way. And you can concentrate on getting Brian better."

"No. You have to go get tested first. Don't just leave. God forbid you have it and then have to take care of Zoe all on your own while you're sick." Aubrey cleared her throat and took another sip of cocoa. "Actually, since Zoe is sleeping, maybe you should go get tested now? If she wakes up while you're gone, I can get her up and give her a bottle. It's the urgent care center next to the grocery store in town. You know the one?"

I shook my head no. We had gone to the grocery store in person only once since I'd gotten here. I'd never noticed an urgent care.

"I'll text you the address. You should get going," she said wearily.

I nodded and went to the kitchen to place my mug in the sink, pausing to wash my hands for the upteenth time today. *Please let me be negative.* I imagined my prayer floating up to the sky and evaporating before reaching any type of "God." I didn't even know if I believed in a God anymore. *Where have you been while all of these people are dying?* The only God I knew was scary and mean. A God of rules and isolation from the rest of the world. Sort of like Covid.

****

"My rapid test came back negative too." The two cups of coffee I had purchased were balanced precariously against my torso as I pulled the door closed. Zoe squealed when she saw me, raising her arms to be picked up.

"Hold on, baby girl. Mommy has to change and wash up first." I brought the cups into the kitchen with me, setting them on the counter. I had already wiped them down in the car. After washing my hands, I peeked my head into the living room.

"Do you mind watching her for one more minute while I go change my clothes? I am so scared of picking up something from urgent care. Do you want me to throw a load of laundry in?"

"Sure. That would be great. I threw my stuff in the hall hamper earlier. Thanks."

"Oh here, I grabbed you a latte." I handed the cup to Aubrey before heading up the stairs.

Aubrey and Brian's bedroom door was closed. The upstairs was quiet, but I could hear Zoe babbling away from the living room. I thought of how happy she seemed to be here. Would she get lonely with just me for company back at the tiny house? My plans to go home were temporarily thwarted while I waited for the results of my other Covid test. We would at least be here for a few more days. But what about Aubrey? What if she ended up having Covid or getting really sick while she was trying to take care of Brian? There was no good solution.

I carried the laundry down to the basement. Aubrey's basement was nice. It wasn't what I would call *finished* but at least it wasn't scary. I thought back to the variety of the basements I'd frequented over the years. Something about basements always creeped me out. Obviously, a derelict, unfinished type of basement, one that was full of, let's say, mannequins or clowns, that was one thing. But even a less typical horror-movie basement filled me with a special kind of dread. I'd thought about this a lot over the years. I knew my traumas. None of them included basements, that I could recall. But for some reason, they all skeeved me out.

Flipping on as many lights as I could find, I allowed my gaze to travel to each corner of Aubrey's now well-lit dwelling. Brian had converted half of it into what could only be described as a man-cave. The entire cement floor was covered with cheap mock tiles. Brian's side, the one opposite the washer and dryer, was covered with a plush black throw rug. Against one wall was a worn leather couch. The cushions were cracked and faded, leaving the formerly dark brown material reminiscent of a huge molasses cookie. A workbench stood alongside the connecting wall.

Above the workbench, a large board had been erected. About a dozen tools hung from hooks attached to the board. One tool was missing, as evidenced by the outline of a saw carefully drawn directly below the hook. Something about the tools on the wall unnerved me. My shoulders hunched, and I felt goosebumps forming along my arms. I held my breath as I studied the other tools. Upon closer inspection, each of the hanging tools had drawn outlines around their figures. I guess that was one way of making sure everything went back to the right place. I bristled at some blip of a memory at the corner of my consciousness but pushed it away and crossed to the other side of the room.

Standing by the washer, I threw in a load of colored clothes. Dumping in more detergent than necessary, I turned the temperature to hot and hoped that if Covid germs had accumulated there, the heat and soap would get rid of them. As I quickly made my way toward the stairs, I paused before ascending. Glancing at the other half of the basement, I marveled at the craftsmanship in the additional shelving Brain had constructed.

He'd build storage shelves spanning the length of the remaining wall. If it wasn't for the misshapen cardboard boxes and overflowing plastic bins lining the shelves, it would look like he'd built two sets of bunk beds without the mattresses. Something felt wrong. My body and head didn't seem to want to function together. A wave of nausea washed over me. The furnace clicked on as I made my way back up the stairs into the warmth of the living room.

"Everything okay?" Aubrey asked. Her gaze settled on my face as I stared at her in silence for a moment.

"What? Oh, um. Yeah. I think maybe I'm getting a migraine." I rubbed my eyes, hoping the halo forming around each image would dissipate.

"Oh, really? I thought the new injection your doctor gave you was helping. How often are you still getting them?" The kindness in her voice made me start to tear up. One of the things I hated most about the migraines was how weepy they made me feel. It was as if the volume of life had been turned up way too high. Every light, sound, and even every emotion, good or bad, seemed to hurt. I recalled the first time I'd been told I was too sensitive. I'd been eight years old. I could still clearly see myself standing in the hallway outside of my classroom. I had almost no memory of my life before age ten, but I remembered this moment in second grade.

"You cry too much," my teacher admonished me. I'd come out of the bathroom crying after two of my least favorite classmates had stolen my shoes and thrown one of them into the toilet.

"You shouldn't let the kids tease you so much. It only makes things worse. If you cry when they are mean, they will only work harder to make you cry more." she'd said.

Yet, as much as I tried to keep my tears to myself over the years, I'd never mastered the art of it. Any time I felt sick or got a migraine, I cried. When I got angry, I cried. Even when I noticed too much beauty in the world around me, I cried. It was as if all of my emotions were housed underneath the finest layer of skin, and a simple brush of a silk sleeve would cause them to erupt.

"Do you want to go lie down for a bit? I can watch Zoe." Aubrey was already sitting beside her on the living room rug. Eve lay panting nearby.

"Are you sure you don't mind?"

She nodded at me as she handed Zoe another toy. "Maybe a nap will help. We'll be fine."

"Thank you. I'll take something for the pain and be back down in a bit." I turned away as I felt an intrusive tear slip down my cheek. Each step felt Herculean as my vision dimmed and my head throbbed. When I finally made my way up to the guest room, I pulled my purse onto the bed with me and scrounged around for my pill box. Locating one of the small blister packs, I pulled the corner of the silver paper back and slipped the wafer onto my tongue. The milky blob melted as I ignored my disbelief and prayed it would work.

****

By the time I came back downstairs, it was dark. Aubrey was in her pajamas, curled up on the couch. She set the book down and patted the cushion next to her.

"I put Zoe to bed for you. She drank all of her bottle and was rubbing her eyes and yawning. I hope that's okay." She leaned forward to grab her wine glass from the coffee table.

"Want some?" I shook my head. Migraines and alcohol didn't mix well.

"Thank you. But she's not in my room. Where'd you put her?"

Aubrey giggled. Clearly, this wasn't her first glass of wine.

"Don't freak out. She's totally safe. She's on a folded-up comforter in the bathtub."

"The tub?" I stood and swayed slightly before plopping back down onto the couch.

"I couldn't put her in my room because of Brian, and I wanted to let you get some sleep. She can't roll off or climb out. She's safe and sound asleep."

I wanted to run upstairs and scoop my baby up and cuddle her. But Aubrey was probably right. She should be safe. Besides, I didn't want to appear ungrateful.

"I made a frozen pizza earlier. Would you like some?" She flipped a bit of the blanket on her lap over my legs and returned her empty glass to the table.

"Not right now, thanks. I'm still a bit nauseous. Thanks again for taking care of Zoe."

"No problem. Brian's staying in bed, and when I checked on him, I wore a mask and washed my hands before touching anything else." We were both worried about catching his Covid. It was kind of miraculous we hadn't gotten sick yet. Right after Brian's test came back positive, Aubrey and I had gotten to work disinfecting the house with alcohol wipes. We wiped down every surface, doorknob, and light switch. I secretly enjoyed every minute of it.

"I've been thinking. I think Zoe and I should go back home. I don't mean to bail now that Brian's sick, but I'm not sure it's the best idea for us to stay." I paused to study her face for any change in expression. She slid her gaze to her lap and remained silent.

"Aub? Will you be okay?"

She nodded, but I could see when she looked up she was struggling to hold back tears.

"What's wrong? I thought that it would be easier on you if we left. I mean, as long as you stay healthy and Brian is okay."

"No, I know. That makes total sense. You don't want to risk Zoe getting sick." She swiped a rapidly falling tear away from her cheek. "It's just been so nice to have you here. And Zoe. It's been a welcome distraction."

Her quiet laugh was full of pain. I waited for her to continue.

"I don't know if you could tell, but things with Brian haven't been great."

I rebuked myself for not noticing. Prior to getting sick, he'd spent much of his day working upstairs. But when he came down for lunch or dinner, he seemed pleasant enough. We'd even spent a few nights hanging out, playing board games, and drinking. I'd never even noticed any tension between them.

"I'm sorry, Aub. What's been going on?" I thought back to several years ago when Aubrey showed up in the middle of the night at my front door. She'd brought a bottle of wine and a tear-stained face as she relayed how he'd been cheating on her. They'd been dating on and off for two years, and she was heartbroken. He'd responded with a promise of fidelity and a pair of diamond earrings.

"It's complicated," she said. I followed her into the kitchen with the empty wine glasses. She started to fill the sink with soapy water and began to wash the food-crusted plates stacked on the counter. When she was upset, she always started cleaning. I grabbed a clean towel from the drawer and began to dry.

What is going on? I swallowed my impatience and waited in silence for her to continue.

"A few years ago, we decided to open up our marriage."

"What?" I nearly dropped the glass I had been wiping down. "What does that mean, *open up?* like sleeping with other people?" There was so much more I wanted to ask, but I held my tongue and hoped she'd continue.

A few years ago? How did I not know this?

"Brian is bisexual."

I stared at her in silence, not knowing what I was supposed to do. Comfort her?

"Aub, I'm so sorry." I reached in front of her and shut the water off. "I mean, can we sit down and talk about this? How are you? Did you suspect he might be gay before you got married?"

She followed me to the kitchen table, grabbing two mugs and the basket of tea bags. I quickly doubled back to fill the kettle and then pulled out the chair beside her.

"He suspected it when we were dating. He said he was curious but never really wanted to pursue anything with anyone else. I mean, until Toby."

"Toby? You mean the affair he had years ago? All this time, I thought Toby was a woman!"

She offered me a sad smile, shaking her head.

"Oh my God. Aub. I am so sorry."

"No, it's fine. I mean, it's okay. We went through a rough patch, but things are actually not horrible right now. We've learned a lot about each other, and we are closer than we ever have been. I know it must sound bizarre. It's certainly not traditional. He and I tell each other everything. And as far as I know, he has never cheated on me since. Things are different now."

"In what way?" I rose to grab the kettle, pouring the steaming warmth into each mug.

She continued. "A few years ago, Brian got really depressed. His doctor put him on some medication, but it didn't really seem to help all that much. After a lot of coaxing, he told me he couldn't stop thinking about being with a man. He felt so guilty just thinking about it. It was overwhelming him. He was drinking a lot, sleeping a lot, and I suspect he was hurting himself."

"Hurting himself?"

"Cutting. I found this little bag tucked away behind the towels in the bathroom cupboard. When I asked him about it, everything kind of came out at once."

I really wanted to ask more about the bag. Despite the shock of what she was telling me, I felt a new sort of kinship with Brian. I had a bag of my own hidden away. I had never spoken of it to anyone. It was something I'd done often as a kid, although I almost never used it now. There was a type of comfort just knowing the option was there.

"Anyway, after lots of talking, crying, some

fighting…we decided to open things up. To see if he could meet someone and date them on the side. He loves me and wants to stay together. He just needs someone in addition to me."

"And you're okay with that?" I winced at the judgment in my tone. "I mean, how do you actually feel?" She surprised me with a tiny grin.

"I am okay actually. I mean, it took some time to adjust. But everything was above board. No hiding. No lying. He told me everything. And, he told me that I could date someone too."

My phone buzzed, and a spark of adrenaline snaked its way from my belly to my chest. I resisted the urge to pull it out and peek at the screen. How many secrets do we all keep from each other?

The friend I thought I knew so well had just become a whole heck of a lot more interesting.

I stared at her in silence. My mind was whirling with questions, yet I felt I would come across as a naive jerk if I asked the wrong ones.

"It's called polyamory. Loving more than one person," she said.

"So, he's in love with someone else?"

She shook her head.

"No, I am."

I sat back, stunned into silence. This had taken an even stranger turn. Brian was gay? Aubrey was in love with someone else? *I really don't know you at all. Then again, there's still a lot you don't know about me.* Topping my tea off with too much sugar, I studied my spoon as I swirled the murky liquid in my mug. Not wanting to say the wrong thing. I remained silent.

"You think I'm a horrible person, don't you?" Her

eyes were bright with tears as I looked into her face.

"No." I shook my head. "I think you might be the bravest person I know."

Chapter Seventeen

July 4, 2020

My belly was huge. Even surrounded by pillows, there was no way to get comfortable. Usually, my makeshift couch in my tiny house was my favorite place to be, but I was restless. My lower back ached. My feet were swollen. I felt like a hot air balloon filled with lead. Everything felt heavy and tenuous. Usually, I was able to keep my space fairly cool with the cross-breeze from all of the windows, but the air was stifling, and I was miserable.

A knock at the front door startled me out of my pity party.

Who the heck is here? I haven't ordered anything to be delivered, and all of my friends knew to contact me before just stopping by. The knocking continued. I hauled myself off of the couch and lumbered to the door. Outside stood a god of a man. *Perhaps he was a mirage?* He held an unlit sparkler in one hand and a store-bought lemonade in the other. He smiled at me through the upper half of my now open door, and took a few steps back before speaking.

"I hope I didn't scare you. I'm your neighbor, Cody. You met my little brother the other day. My mom is the neighborhood midwife?" His voice rose slightly at the end of his sentence as if he was waiting for me to shut the door in his face.

"Oh." I pushed open the door and stepped onto my front step. He took another step back and set the lemonade and firecracker down on the ground and pulled the fabric face mask dangling from around his neck up over his mouth and nose.

"Do you want me to wear this? I didn't think you'd appreciate a strange man in a mask coming to your door unannounced."

"It's okay. I think we are all right outside. Unless you want me to wear one?" I was hoping he would say no since I honestly didn't even know where I had left mine. I rarely left my house, even before all of this crazy Covid stuff. I had very little reason to. *Don't cover up that gorgeous face.* The thought popped into my head before I could stop it.

Acutely aware I was the size of a small whale, I tugged at the hem of my shorts. Luckily, I had decided to put a bra on this morning. I'd finally succumbed to buying some ugly nursing bras after breaking the clasp of my favorite bra while trying to squish my ever-growing boobs into it.

"Sorry for my appearance." I motioned down to my clothing. "I was cleaning."

"You look beautiful." The words spilled out of his mouth, reddening his chiseled face. "I'm sorry, that was forward of me. I tend to say what I'm thinking before filtering." He laughed. "Sam told me you were pretty. He was right."

Charm oozed from this guy's pores, and as he smiled again, a tiny dimple appeared on his right cheek. *My melting heart.*

"I'm sorry, who's Sam?"

"My little brother. He gave you my mom's info? She's the midwife?" He studied me.

"Oh, right. *Sam.* He was sweet. Your mom's name is Marilyn, right?"

He nodded.

"So, um, is there something I can help you with?" I leaned my aching back against the doorframe. "Or, do you just have a thing for pregnant women?" I eyed the sweating lemonade propped in the dirt by the step.

He laughed again. "I actually do have a thing for pregnant women, I guess. Probably growing up around all of those home births I followed my mom to. My life has been filled with pregnant women."

My eyebrows raised.

"I mean, not to say that *I* got them pregnant. Not that I couldn't get them pregnant if I, I mean if they wanted me to…Um, I'm just gonna stop talking now."

He reached for the lemonade and began transferring the sweating bottle back and forth between his hands. Part of me wanted to go back inside and lock the door, but a bigger part of me was fascinated by this hot guy standing on my front step making a fool of himself.

What did this guy really want? Is he a creeper?

"Actually, my mom sent me over to introduce myself and see if you needed anything." He cleared his throat and continued. "She was going to come by to meet you, but one of her clients just went into labor. She said she can stop over in a few days if that's all right with you."

"Oh." A smidge of disappointment crept down my spine. Was he leaving already? I didn't realize how lonely I'd become for human company until he showed up, reminding me I was still part of an actual society. Reminding me just because I was about to pop out a baby didn't mean I shouldn't jump his bones. *What is wrong with me? I just met this guy. He could be a mass murderer for all I know! Look at what happened to you the last time you slept with a random stranger!* I took a deep breath and waited for reason to set it.

"Thank you. It was really nice of you to stop by and introduce yourself." *I hope I sound more mature than I feel right now. I feel like a squirming middle schooler with her first crush.*

"It's no problem. It's a beautiful day for a walk." he bent to pick up the sparkler and then held both items out to me. "I brought you a cold drink and a little celebratory stick for Independence Day."

I burst into laughter. "A celebratory stick? That isn't even in the least bit subtle." I laughed again but quieted when I saw how red his face had become.

"I didn't mean…no, I just…" He rubbed his wrinkled brow.

"It's okay. I'm sorry. It just sounded funny." I stifled a giggle.

"I didn't mean it that way." He grinned. "Although…" He paused when he saw me raise my eyebrows. "Um, our family always lights them before the firework show. I just thought you might like one. We have a case of them."

"Most definitely," I replied. "Thank you."

He handed me the gifts and stood awkwardly in the dirt. The July heat pricked at my skin. All I wanted to do was sit and drink this sugary goodness.

He turned to go, then hesitated and spun back around.

"Would you like to go for a walk sometime? I mean, I know you don't know me, but maybe after you meet my mom? When you find out from her I'm a decent guy? I promise I'm not a serial killer. Just a decent, awkward, single guy from the neighborhood who tends to talk too much."

"Do you always have your mom vouch for you? How old are you anyway?"

"Twenty-five."

Three years younger than me. Not too bad. Hopefully, he was more mature than he looked. I'd have pegged him for much younger. Does he still live with his mom? God, I hope not. What was I getting myself into? Maybe life out here was a bit lonelier than I wanted to admit to myself.

"Sure. A walk would be nice. Maybe a short one? On a cooler day?"

He nodded.

"Want my number?" he asked. "You could text me when you're feeling like getting out for a bit?"

"Yeah, okay. Hold on." I brought the gifts inside and set them on the counter. Grabbing my phone, I returned to the front step. I started to hand it to him, then suddenly pulled it back to my chest.

"Do you mind just telling me your number, and I'll put it in myself? I'm assuming you don't have Covid, but I'm a bit of a germaphobe."

He nodded and told me his number as I entered it into my contacts, under the name *hott celebratory stick*. I felt my cheeks redden as I held a giggle in.

"Text me anytime," he said as he began slowly walking backward down the path. "I'm bored out of my mind since losing my job. So whenever you're free, I'll probably be free for a walk…or whatever." He turned, and I watched him walk away.

What the heck had just happened? Did an amazingly gorgeous man really just come up to my tiny house and hit on me? Absurd. I studied his number on my screen and clicked on the icon to send him a message.

—Thanks for the celebratory stick. 8-) Willow.—

****

May 6, 2021

Aubrey cleared away the tea cups, and I followed her back to the couch. Questions swirled in my mind. *Who is this person she's in love with? How could I not have known?* We sat down on the couch. Brian was upstairs, coughing. A reminder that I shouldn't be here. I should take Zoe and go home. We need to stay healthy. Hospitals were flooded with people dying from this invisible murderer. Aubrey interrupted my mental catastrophizing.

"I hope you don't think badly of me." She pulled a pillow onto her lap and began playing with the decorative tassles.

"Of course not. I'm super curious, though. Who is this person? Where did you meet him?" I paused. "Is it a *him*?"

Her laughter lightened the density in the air.

"Yes, it's a *him*. His name is Rex. I met him online."

Rex? Online? I waited for her to continue.

"It took me a while to take the plunge, but a few months after Brian suggested I try to meet someone, I joined a dating app for married people."

I'm so naive. I didn't even know there was such a

thing.

"I had started reading up on polyamory and non-traditional lifestyles. Hooking up isn't my style. I was curious, and Brian was really encouraging. We talked a lot, I mean, long-ass conversations deep into the night about our relationship, about our future. We both wanted to stay together."

Nodding, I tried to keep the expression on my face open and kind. She could read my face like a book she'd memorized as a child. Despite all the questions orbiting my gray matter, I didn't want her to think I was judging her.

"There are a lot of creepers out there. But Rex was different. He's married too, and his wife is on board with it. We started chatting, and it just kinda developed into a relationship."

"So, you've met him?"

"Well, not in person. He lives really far away. And then Covid happened. So…no." Her voice was wistfully sad.

"But you've video chatted with him? Like, you *know* he's a real person?" The judgment was creeping into my voice despite my best attempts at remaining neutral. "Where does he live?"

"Phoenix. And yes, we have video chatted. He is a real person."

More coughing could be heard from upstairs.

"I'm gonna go check on Brian. I'll be right back." Aubrey grabbed the cloth mask from the coffee table and pulled it on as she exited the room. We'd known each other for most of our lives, and I'd always considered her the more conservative out of the two of us. Unlike me, she was still heavily involved in the church. Prior to Covid, she and Brian went every Sunday. She volunteered at the food cupboard there. A fun night out for Aubrey consisted of a trip to a bookstore and, if she was really feeling risque, a double shot of espresso. Now I could see that I was the more boring of the two of us.

Sure, I'd had a one-nighter and managed to get myself knocked up, but that seemed mild compared to being in love with two men. Then again, I had my secrets too. Secrets I was not planning on sharing, even with her. I didn't ever want to risk losing Zoe. Every moment with her was a gift that could be taken away in an instant. Just like that song about a thief in the night, a stranger could show up and demand to take her back. No matter how much I deluded myself, she didn't really belong to me. Her biological mother was out there somewhere, and could show up at any moment to snatch her away. I reached out for my wine glass and gulped down the final swig as Aubrey came back into the room.

"So, are you going to meet this Rex guy in person?" My curiosity wouldn't let me wait for her to sit down before questioning her.

"Not anytime soon." She sighed. "And who knows how long this whole Covid thing will last."

"Right." I nodded. "Speaking of…how's Brian?"

"He seems pretty miserable. He slept for a bit, but his cough keeps waking him up. He's running a fever, but I'm sure he'll be fine."

Another bout of coughing from upstairs drifted our way.

"His cough doesn't sound good. Do you think you should bring him to the doctor or something?"

She shook her head. "His primary said there isn't much they can do right now. And to only bring him into the hospital if he is having a hard time breathing."

We sat in silence for a moment. I hoped it wouldn't come to that. More coughing could be heard from upstairs.

Aubrey stared into her wine glass silently, while my mind raced with unspoken words.

"Do you want to watch a movie or something?" I reached for the remote.

"Actually, I'm feeling kinda wiped out. I think I'm gonna turn in."

"Oh, of course. I'll head upstairs so you can crash on the couch." I stood and began to pull out the linens she'd folded neatly beside the arm of the couch.

"No it's okay. I actually just really want to sleep in my own bed tonight. The couch isn't all that comfortable for sleeping on." I raised my eyebrows, about to object.

"Besides, I want to keep an eye on Brian."

Covid, Covid, Covid my brain repeated. *She's gonna catch Covid. I have to get out of here.* I cleared my throat and resisted the urge to remind her of what a bad idea that was.

"Do you think you'll be able to sleep with Brian's coughing? I can stay down here if you want to use the bed in your guest room. Zoe should sleep through the night." *It's time for us to go.* I thought.

"No, don't be silly. I have noise-canceling headphones I use them all the time to drown out his snoring." She laughed. "We'll be fine."

I studied her face in the dim light of the living room. She did look tired. Her furrowed brow gave away the fact she was worried. I wanted to ask her more about how she was feeling, but I gave her a nod and a smile as she quietly walked away.

I wasn't tired enough to go to bed yet, so I flipped the TV on and pulled the afghan across my lap. I must have dozed off during another marathon of reality TV because Aubrey's running down the stairs startled me awake.

"What's wrong?" I bolted upright as she ran into the room. *Is Zoe okay? I should go check on her.*

"My phone! Did I leave it down here? Brian isn't breathing right!" She pushed the magazines, mugs, and wine glasses on the coffee table aside as she rummaged around for her phone.

"Use mine. Here." I stood as it plopped to the floor, having been lodged somewhere under the afghan with me.

"Will you call 911? I'm going to go back up to sit with him."

"Of course. Is he breathing? Does he need CPR?" I hoped I could remember what to do.

"He's breathing, but he can't get full breaths. His color isn't right. Call them and let them in, okay?"

"Calling now." I followed her to the bottom of the staircase as she ran up and I dialed.

After giving them all the information I had, I unlocked the door, flipped on the porch light, and ran upstairs to check on Zoe. She was still sound asleep. *What a gift to be able to sleep through such noise.* I ducked back into the guest room and pulled out the white noise machine I'd brought with me. I plugged it in and cranked up the volume as the sound of ocean waves and lullabies filled the space. Tiptoeing out, I pulled the door closed and peaked in on Aubrey and Brian.

She sat on the bed beside him, speaking softly and rubbing his chest. Brian was propped up against several pillows. His face looked grayish as he leaned forward, trying to catch his breath. I ran back down the stairs and stood by the window to watch for the lights. Within minutes they appeared, sirens silenced. An ambulance, followed by a fire truck, pulled up to the house as I opened the door and waved them inside.

"They are upstairs," I said in greeting.

Two stocky masked men in uniform nodded to me as they quickly walked past me with large duffel bags. The back door of the ambulance opened, and a woman with long, colorful dreadlocks hopped out. She pulled a yellow metal gurney out and set another bag on top of it. Her web of hair was caught under the strap of one of the large bags she carried. She sighed and readjusted the strap, sweeping the colorful strands aside as she made her way to the door.

"Do you need help?" I tried to flatten myself against the wall, not sure what to do. Wanting to be helpful without getting in the way.

"I'm good." Her voice was slightly muffled through her mask. She paused to look around. "Mind if I leave this here in case we need it?"

I nodded and motioned for her to come in. The fire truck sat silently as she made her way past me and up the stairs. Eve barked at the intruders and ran up and down the stairs causing even more commotion. I called her over, but she ignored me and continued barking. Pushing the front door closed, I went to the kitchen and grabbed a dog cookie from the glass jar on the counter.

As soon as she heard me lift the lid, she appeared. I grabbed her, tucking her under one arm while I deposited her and the cookie into the downstairs bathroom.

More feet clomped down the stairs as the woman and one of the men brought the stretcher past me and up the stairs. I could hear Zoe crying in the distance, and my heart dropped as I knew I couldn't make my way up there to comfort her. Once the stairs were clear, I raced back up to the guest room and eased the door open to my snot-nosed, red-faced, angry child.

She quieted as soon as she saw me and raised her arms to be picked up.

"Mmm," she cooed, wiping her wet face against my shoulder. I could hear talking and movement from the hallway and peeked out to see if I could get by. Brian was on the stretcher. An oxygen mask covered his face. Zoe clung to me as I stood in the doorway, hoping to catch a glimpse of Aubrey. Pale-faced, she followed everyone down the hall toward the stairs.

"Aub," I said as she turned to me. Her eyes were full of fear.

"Is he going to be okay?"

She began to cry, nodding her head and shrugging her shoulders at the same time.

"They are taking him to the hospital to help him breathe better. But they won't let me go with him." She sobbed.

"What? Why?" Zoe was wide awake now and reached for Aubrey. It was as if she knew that she needed comforting. I shifted her to my other hip, which felt completely wrong, so I quickly shifted her back.

"Covid. They said no one else is allowed in. I have

179

to stay here and do paperwork and stuff. Someone from the hospital intake is going to call me as soon as they get him there. My phone! I have to find my phone." She followed them down the steps. Once they were all on the ground floor, I took Zoe downstairs into the kitchen. I thought I had remembered seeing Aubrey's phone charging in the kitchen. I unplugged it and brought it to her.

"Thanks." She tucked it into her robe and followed the paramedics into the dim morning. A sliver of moon still graced the pale sky. Aubrey stood crying as they loaded Brian into the back of the ambulance. She reached out to touch his shoeless foot before they closed the door. Zoe squealed as a sobbing Aubrey returned to the house.

"He's going to be okay. They will take good care of him." My words sounded hollow as I watched her tear-stained face. She slumped onto the couch, pulling out her phone and grasping it tightly.

I set Zoe on the floor, propping her up with random pillows from the couch. She wanted to sit up, but every once in a while, her balance would falter and she'd tip over. She should be sleeping. But she was wide awake and ready to play. I handed her a rattle and sat next to Aubrey.

"He'll be okay," I repeated.

She stared at her phone as if willing it to ring. Eve barked from the bathroom, and I stood to let her outside into the slowly brightening dawn.

Chapter Eighteen

May 9, 2021

The next three days were a blur. I tried to support Aubrey the best way that I knew how. But I only ended up feeling like I kept getting in the way. She still wasn't allowed into the hospital to see him, and the stress of the situation was turning her into a different person.

"I can't take this anymore," she sobbed. Eve jumped up on her lap, and Zoe looked up from the blanket I had spread for her on the floor.

"I'm just going to go over there and demand they let me see him. I can't stand the fact he's all alone."

"I'm so sorry, Aub." Brian was now in the makeshift ICU. He was on a ventilator and was being sedated. The nurse had called her this morning with an update, and things were finally looking a bit better.

"He's still on a lot of meds and is asleep most of the time. So, I guess that's good." Her eyes were rimmed with red, and her nose was chapped from the constant crying.

"He's strong. He's going to get better." Last night I caught Aubrey sobbing in front of the news. It seemed like the news coverage was only about Covid. All of the deaths. The overcrowded hospitals. The overworked doctors and nurses. I quickly turned it off and took the remote away from her.

"Didn't they tell you this morning that they are going to try to wean him off the ventilator?" She nodded tearfully.

"So, we give them time to do their jobs. They are going to help him get better. He'll be back home before you know it." Hopefully, I sounded more upbeat than I felt. Of course, I wanted Brian to recover and return home. My pessimistic nature had already assumed he was going to die. I pushed the dark thought away. *Home.* I was ready to go home. But leaving now wasn't an option. I had to wait and hope that Brian would survive.

****

Another agonizing week went by before Aubrey was finally told that Brian was well enough to return home. He was off of the ventilator and had been moved to a *stepdown* unit, where they kept trying to prepare for his return home. He was still on oxygen, but a physical therapist had gotten him out of bed to try walking a few feet out by the nurse's station. He was fatigued easily and frequently out of breath, so rather than calling Aubrey, he texted. The first time he texted her from the hospital, she bounded into the kitchen, squealing with delight.

"Ohmygodohmygodohmygod!" she yelled as she jumped up and down.

I'd been feeding Zoe some swampy-looking rice cereal, which she promptly spit out with a gooey grin.

"What's going on?" I tried to wipe the mess away from Zoe's face but only succeeded in spreading it around further.

"It's Brian!" She held up her phone, her face beaming. "He texted me!"

"I'm so glad to hear he's feeling well enough to text you, Aub. What did he say?" I bent to retrieve a plastic toy bear Zoe kept throwing to the ground.

"How is he doing? Any chance he can come home soon?" *So, I can go home too?* I thought, guiltily. My mind raced as I thought of all the stress Aubrey must be feeling, mixed with my desire to return to the solace of our tiny home.

"He got out of bed and walked a few feet today! Of course, he had to bring a portable oxygen tank with him, but he thinks once he needs a bit less oxygen throughout the day, they will send him home!"

"How soon will that be?"

"His doctor said if all goes well, he might be able to come home in a day or two."

Zoe threw the plastic bear to the floor again. She pulled her bib off and signed for me to pick her up. I wiped her face and hands again and set her on the floor to play. I pulled open a lower cupboard and grabbed a large metal bowl for her. She immediately began to put the bear in the bowl, then tip it over and laugh as it tumbled out. She giggled at her newest favorite game.

"That's great, Aub!" I studied her flushed face. "Listen, I don't really know the best time to bring this up, but I think it's time for Zoe and me to head back home."

Her smile faded, but she nodded in approval.

"I don't want to bail on you if you need my help with Brian, but I kinda feel like we'll be in the way. We have had a great time visiting. Thank you so much for putting up with us for as long as you have."

"Of course." She walked over to the drawer closest to the sink and rummaged around until she located a worn wooden spoon. She bent to hand it to Zoe, who exuberantly began beating on the bowl. She raised her voice slightly to continue.

"We loved having you here. It was so nice to have you both in our bubble. It's gonna take a while for Brian to recover." Her expression softened, her face momentarily morphing into a version of her mother. "I'm gonna miss you."

"Us too." I reached out and placed my hand on her arm, willing myself to ignore the thought of the germs I was touching. "Do you want me to stay a few more days to help you get Brian settled, or would it be easier if we leave before he gets back?"

She thought for a moment.

"It's up to you. You are welcome to stay as long as you want."

Aubrey and I were chronic people pleasers. As children, we even struggled when it came to making decisions about what to play. Neither one of us wanted the responsibility of disappointing the other. But I was eager to go home, and if we left tomorrow, Aubrey would have a little bit of down time before Brian arrived.

"Would you be upset if we left tomorrow?" I watched her face intently. *Was that an inkling of relief I see?*

She shook her head. "No, I won't be upset. But can we video chat throughout the week?"

"Of course!" I replied.

"You might get sick of hearing from me." she said.

"Never," I said as I made my way over to the sink to wash away the invisible.

****

Zoe's pudgy hand smushed up against Eve's silky fur as I bent, allowing her to say goodbye. Zoe's legs were still wrapped around my middle as she tried to reach the other arm toward the dog.

"Gentle." I crouched down with her, swaying slightly as I regained my balance. My hand reached out to model how to gently pet Eve.

"Say bye-bye." Zoe's fingers began to close around a handful of fur. I quickly pried them open and stood back up.

"Say bye-bye to Auntie Bree." The title I'd just given her seemed to appear from nowhere.

"Aww" she clucked, catching my gaze for a second and smiling.

"Bye-bye, Zoe. Maybe the next time I see you, you'll be walking!" Aubrey's eyes filled with tears. "I'm gonna miss seeing her grow."

I hugged her. "It's not like we live that far away. Just a few hours. Once this Covid thing passes, we can get back to normal life and visit all the time."

Little did I know life would never return to normal.

****

To: Melaniewalker@catharsistimepress.com
From:Willowmorgan666@gmail.com
Subject: Age 13
Mel, Are you okay? I def don't want to be a bother, but you told me to keep sending you my entries. It's been a while since I've heard from you. I tried texting and calling but just got voicemail. Please let me know that you are all right. -W

"Why can't we just be like a normal family?" I whined.

Mr. Calkins stood in the doorway to my room.

Molly had stayed after school to work on her science fair project. I'd come home excited at the prospect of watching my favorite show on TV. Since we didn't have a guide, I'd found out earlier in the week that my favorite prairie-based family TV show would be coming on at four p.m. On the rare occasion that the Calkins let us watch TV, this was on the list of approved shows.

"We do not strive for normalcy." Mr. Calkins sneered. "Be not of this world…" he began.

"I already did my homework," I interrupted him as my heels kicked at the metal bar of my chair leg. The sharp sting of pain assaulted me with each swift kick. It reminded me I was still alive, even if a part of me felt dead inside.

"Did you read your Bible?" he cleared his throat.

I nodded. Maybe there was hope. Maybe I could watch it after all!

"How long?" he asked

"Huh?"

"How long did you read your Bible for?"

"I dunno. I read it before breakfast like you told me to." The tang of teenage hatred pooled in the back of my mouth.

"It's God that is telling you, Willow. Not me."

Kick. Kick. Kick.

He waited for me to say more. But I knew if I opened my mouth, nothing good would come out.

"How long is the show?"

"I dunno, maybe like an hour?"

"Then you need to read an hour of the Bible before you watch television."

An hour! My friend Rachel had been watching the

re-runs all week. Today was supposed to be the episode right after the oldest sister went blind! I'd already missed my favorite episode, the one where she actually lost her vision, but I was eager to re-follow the storyline of her going away to the special school. Of course, the best part about the school was the hot male teacher. I had to assume that she eventually falls in love with him, as I hadn't yet seen any additional episodes.

In real life dating was strictly forbidden, so this teacher was the closest I would get to any sort of stirring of my *sinful* loins. My crush wasn't solely on the teacher, though. I was also obsessed with the father. Not in a romantic way. Rather, in the "I wish you were my father" kind of way.

My daydreams were frequently filled with absurd scenarios where I would be milking the cows on a sultry day, and he would lovingly clomp into the barn with his manly work boots to bring me a cool glass of homemade lemonade. He'd place his calloused hand on top of my head, and I would feel what I imagined to be fatherly love surrounding me with happiness. Then, of course, he would leave the barn, and the hunky local neighbor boy would grace me with his muscley presence.

"But it starts in fifteen minutes!" I protested hyper-aware that anything sounding remotely like an attitude creeping into my tone would be met with punishment.

"We are starting a new rule. The Bible Bank. We must always put God first. He is a jealous God and created us for His pleasure. He needs to know He is always your top priority and that everything you do is for his glory."

He stared up at the ceiling while spewing his

version of truth. Did he just make up this crap on the spot?

"Read an hour of the Bible for every hour of TV you want to watch. If you prepare right, you can watch tomorrow."

Kick. Kick. Kick. It hurt so good.

Chapter Nineteen

May 9, 2021

Zoe slept through the entire ride home, which was perfect. She still wasn't a fan of the car seat, but after a few minutes of kicking her feet and whining, she quieted and nodded off. As soon as I put the car into "park" in my dirt driveway, she woke up. My tiny home beckoned to me as I threw my car door open. Opening the back door, I unlatched Zoe from the seat and lifted her to me. No sense in bringing the car seat inside with us. I doubted we would be going anywhere any time soon. She clung to me fiercely as I bent slightly to retrieve my bag from the back seat and failed at slinging it over my shoulder. Letting it slide down to the ground, I left it beside the car as Zoe and I approached the door. My laptop was in the bag, so I made a mental note to come back and grab it soon.

The house was stuffy and the air stale. My uncle had been kind enough to collect my mail and deposit it on the countertop for me. A stack of glossy landfill lay unopened, and I sighed at the prospect of going through it. Looking around my small space filled me with peace. My plants had been well cared for in my absence, and from my vantage point, I could see almost all of my favorite items I'd placed throughout my home.

Zoe signed to be let down, and I set her gently on the handmade rug by the couch. I'd made the rug out of several pairs of old jeans I'd cut into strips and knit together. It was a bit atrocious looking, but I loved it anyway. Now that she could basically sit properly on her own, I'd have to start thinking about baby-proofing even more. Soon enough, she would be crawling. The living room was pretty much free of any hazards, so I took a few steps back into the kitchen to grab a bowl and some spoons for her to play with. After setting them on the lumpy rug with her, I dashed up to my loft to check on Matilda. Matilda was an old spider plant given to me years ago. Back when I lived with the Calkins, Angel had brought me a small clipping of the plant in a red plastic cup. Molly and I followed her directions to keep it in the shallow water until roots formed and then placed it in a pot with soil. Matilda followed me from makeshift home to makeshift home, and I even managed to keep her alive during the two weeks I'd lived out of my rusty car. She was full and lush and took up residence in the corner by my bed.

I smoothed out the edge of my comforter as my thoughts were interrupted by a knocking at the door. Running down the stairs, I was relieved to see that Zoe was busy gumming up my wooden spoon with drool from her spot on the rug. Resisting the urge to ignore the knock, I peeked through the tiny eyehole I'd drilled in the front door. My heart sped up as I pulled the door open.

Cody stood in the sunlight. He held a face mask in one hand and my bag in the other.

"Forget something?" he grinned.

"Have you been lurking in the bushes waiting for

my return?" I cautiously laughed.

The texting we'd been doing during my trip to Aubrey's felt free and easy and exciting. Even though I wanted to, I hadn't really told Aubrey about Cody yet. Keeping whatever this was to myself not only felt safer but added to the excitement of the new relationship energy. I swallowed down my nervousness at seeing him in person after all this while. I was never one for getting my hopes up, for fear of getting hurt. Becoming close via text was still a lot different than in person. Part of me wanted to run over and hug him, but a bigger part held me frozen in place.

He studied me for a moment. His gaze lingered on my face. I tugged at my sweatshirt, wishing I'd dressed less like a homeless middle-aged woman, and more like the MILF he claimed to see me as. My middle still sported baby weight, and I'd taken to wearing oversized clothing to hide it.

"You told me what time you were leaving Aubrey's, so I deduced what time you'd return." he handed me the bag. "It was easier than lurking in the bushes. Although I admit, it's a bit less romantic."

"Romantic? More like creepy." I smirked.

We stared at each other until Zoe's make-shift drum reminded me of her presence. *Should I let him in? Make him wear a mask? Should I wear a mask?* My thoughts whirled as I stared at the mask in his hand.

"Do you want me to put this on?" He lifted it toward his face, pausing for my answer.

"I dunno. I think maybe *I* should be the one wearing a mask? Since Brian is sick. Honestly, I don't know what to do. The clinic had called me during my ride home, and thankfully my second Covid test was negative. But what if I could carry the virus from Brian on my clothes? Was it in my hair? I made a mental note to shower as soon as possible.

We stared at each other for a moment.

"I don't quite know what to do either. The news seems to say a whole bunch of different things. Wear a mask, don't wear a mask. Stay indoors, stay outdoors. Get vaccinated...."

"Oh, are you getting vaccinated?" He nodded. "My mom signed me up, I got the shot last week. It wasn't bad. I was down for a day or two, no big deal. Look, I won't bother you anymore today. I just wanted to pop over to say welcome back." He took a step backward, and I felt a wave of disappointment wash over me.

"I was wondering..." He began.

"Yes?"

"If I could see Zoe? I mean, just like peek at how big she's gotten? My mom made me promise to report back to her about how cute she is now. She even begged me to take a picture."

"Oh, sure. Just a second." A wave of disappointment washed over me, settling like a stone in the pit of my stomach. I left the door open and picked her up from the rug. She wrapped her legs around my middle, pulling the oversized sweatshirt askew. I could feel one of the shoulders sliding down, exposing the butterfly tattoo below my right collarbone. His gaze followed the slipping fabric, and his eyebrows shot up in surprise.

"She's so big!" He smiled up at Zoe, and she returned the grin. "She's beautiful. Just like her mother." He pulled out his phone. "Would it be creepy to ask to take a pic for my mom?" She's always asking about the two of you."

"I'm not exactly looking my best right now." I suddenly felt shy and even more self-conscious.

"You always look beautiful. But obviously, I won't take your picture if you don't want me to." He started to tuck his phone away.

"No, it's okay. You can take one. Maybe just focus on Zoe instead of me?" Ignoring my previous statement, I tucked my face against her as we both grinned into the camera.

****

"The house feels so empty without you guys." Aubrey's face flitted in and out of frame as I adjusted my laptop.

"How's Brian?" I asked.

"He thinks he might be able to come home tomorrow." She dropped the pen she'd been fidgeting with and disappeared for a second before popping back onto the screen.

"That's great! So, what will you do tonight, now that you have the house all to yourself?"

Aubrey turned her laptop toward the coffee table to show me an unopened bottle of wine. She moved it back and grinned.

"Eve and I are going to chillax on the couch with a bottle of red. I'm gonna binge watch something, and then I plan to sleep in tomorrow. I took the day off of work to clean up the house a bit and pick him up from the hospital."

"Sounds like a nice evening. Listen, I'm sorry to run, but I'm gonna give Zoe a bath and get her ready for bed soon."

"Oh, of course." Aubrey smiled again, but I could

see a wisp of sadness in her eyes. "Give her a kiss from me. I'll text you later."

"Sounds good. But if I don't reply, it probably means I fell asleep." Knowing Aubrey, if I didn't reply, she would freak out a bit and assume I didn't want to talk to her. And even though I wanted a bit of space, I'd learned to buffer my introversion by placating her need for connection.

"Enjoy the quiet. And if you don't hear back from me tonight, I'll text you tomorrow." Even if I was still awake, I wasn't planning on texting anyone. I couldn't wait to slip into my own bed with a good book and not have to interact with another person for a while.

"Okay. Goodnight. Talk later." She raised her wine glass to the camera and ended the video call.

Breathing a sigh of relief, I closed my laptop and turned my attention back to Zoe. Now that we were home, she had a proper highchair to sit in. She'd been busily smushing her pudgy hands through clumps of rice cereal on the tray. Her fingers and face were a mottled mess of whitish goo.

"Come on, baby girl, time for a bath." I picked her up, holding her at arm's length as I carried her to the half-tub. I'd lucked out in finding an old copper utility sink and converting it into a half-tub with a rainfall shower head.

On the rare occasion I wanted a bath; the tub was just large enough for me to sit with my knees bent. It was quite big for Zoe, so I placed a plastic dish pan in the bottom and filled it with warm soapy water. By now my own clothes were speckled with rice cereal as she squirmed on my lap. It was a bit of a comedy routine to get her undressed and into the makeshift tub, but I did it. The calming, gentle aroma of baby shampoo filled the air as I set her in the water. It was so good to be back home.

****

May 11, 2021

"I lied," Cody said as he walked up the dirt driveway.

Zoe and I were enjoying the midday sun. She sat on the quilt I'd dragged from the small storage shed I had behind the house. I'd always considered it a lucky find at last year's church sale.

"Hello to you, too." I smirked and stood up to greet him. Since most of our communication had been via text since I'd met him, it still felt slightly awkward to see him in person.

"What did you lie about?" I picked at my cuticles.

"Giving you space." He crouched down to Zoe's level. "Hi Zoe. Remember me?"

Zoe looked at him and grinned then turned her attention back to the toys in front of her.

"I didn't necessarily say I wanted *space*, just that I was an introvert." Last night, we exchanged a few more texts. I had tried to explain my need for *down-time* during a conversation about how much I loved being back home in my tiny house.

Cody was a major extrovert and simply couldn't seem to grasp my need for alone time. He thrived on social interaction. After losing his job as a physical therapy assistant at the beginning of the pandemic, he admitted that he was secretly happy to move back home. His little brother was always bringing friends around. His mother seemed to bring home a new dinner guest each week, and he and his father hosted a game night every Saturday.

"I also told you I'd text you before just dropping by." I nodded in agreement and gave him a fake frown. "But I was already out for a walk. And before I knew what was happening, my feet just so happened to bring me here."

"Well, since you are one of the few humans I don't abhor, you are welcome." I sat back down on the quilt with Zoe and motioned for him to join us.

"*Tolerating* me isn't exactly a ringing endorsement, but I'll take it." He grinned. "Am I sitting too close? Do you want me to put a mask on?"

I pondered this for a moment. What was the right thing to do? We were outside, which was clearly safer. But the information surrounding Covid protocols was murky and often contradictory.

"I think we're okay. Although, maybe I'm the one who should wear a mask since Brian had Covid."

"But your tests were negative, right?" he asked.

I nodded. "Honestly, I'm not that worried." The lie tripped off my tongue so easily. Of course I was worried. My whole life felt like one big worry. But the battle inside of my head between my obsessive thoughts about germs and my compulsion to avoid them at all costs was often masked by my seeming indifferent. My body would pay the price later on in the form of panic attacks and chronic pain. It was a pattern that I'd grown accustomed to.

I gasped as Zoe tipped from a sitting position toward all fours. She caught herself with one arm and tested out the new half-leaning stance. A moment later, she reverted to laying on her tummy and tried to scooch her way up toward another toy.

"Did you see that? She just recently started crawling!" My heart swelled with pride as I pushed the toy closer to her.

"She's a champ." His dimple brightened his cheek as he grinned.

"Listen," I paused, thinking through how to word this. "I know we've been talking a lot."

"Oh boy." He clicked his tongue. "This doesn't sound good."

"No, no. It's nothing bad. I'm really enjoying getting to know you. I guess I just wanted to make sure you don't feel obligated or anything."

"Obligated?"

"Well, like obligated to be friends with the complicated, lonely single mom." My laugh sounded hollow.

"Are you lonely?" He pressed.

His hand inched toward mine near the edge of the blanket. He let it linger a few inches from my fingertips. I could feel the heat from his hand so close to mine and wondered what it would feel like for him to touch me. I pushed the thought away, forcing myself to look into his ocean blue eyes. The edges were ringed in green.

"No," I lied and moved my hand to my lap.

"Is that what we are, *friends*?"

I could feel his gaze on my face as I looked into my tiny yard. I thought of the rose bushes behind the house and the tiny grave underneath them. We'd flirted over the past several weeks of texting, but none of our conversations had addressed romance.

"I like you." I looked back at him. *Those eyes. Ugh. That dimple. Why did he have to be so darn adorable?*

"But I'm not so great at *relationships*." The word stretched out as I deepened my voice for comedic effect. I tried on a wonky English accent. It didn't fit.

"So what? We'll take it slow." He paused. "If that's what you want."

Suddenly Zoe started to cry. A stink was emanating from her, and she wasn't going to get any happier until I changed her.

"I'm sorry." I scooped her up and held her at arm's length as I wrinkled my nose. "I need to change her."

He stood and followed us to the door. Zoe whimpered and rubbed her eyes.

"Are we done?" irritation crept into his voice.

"No. Not done." I pulled the door open and turned to face him again. Zoe kicked her heels into my hip. "Maybe just starting." Wanting to be the one to *drop the mic*, I sashayed inside turning back toward him.

His face lit up as his dimple made another dashing appearance.

"I've gotta change her and put her down for a nap."

He nodded, still grinning like a naughty schoolboy.

"Text me later?" I grinned. *So much for slow.*

Chapter Twenty

May 13, 2021

Zoe giggled with glee. Her face tipped toward the sun as I pushed her stroller forward. We'd never visited Cody's house, but after a series of texts from his mom inviting us over, I'd finally relented. Marilyn lured me over for some of her famous homemade lemonade, and we'd agreed to stay outdoors and sit far away from each other. She'd even offered to wear a mask, which felt unnecessary.

The map on my phone said their house was less than a mile away, but my legs were already aching. I'd never been in good shape, even before my pregnancy. The burning in my lungs reminded me that I really needed to get out and walk more. The weather was finally warm so I had no excuse.

After stopping several times to retrieve items Zoe had dropped along the way, we finally arrived. The long dirt driveway led to a beautiful yard and an even more magnificent house. My own tiny dwelling paled in comparison. Marilyn pushed open the screen door and made her way down the porch steps.

"Welcome!" Her face exuded happiness and I could see that Cody inherited his dimple from her.

Had she been watching for me from the window?

"Hi," I called, stopping to lift Zoe from the stroller.

She shied away, clinging to me for dear life.

"Look at her! She's so big!" Marilyn cooed, but kept her distance. Besides a few photos I'd sent her, she'd only seen Zoe two or three times since her birth. *What if she can somehow tell that Zoe wasn't mine?* The fear settled into my stomach like a hollow pit.

"Would you like to sit in the garden or on the front porch? Cody will be out in a minute. He's pouring the lemonade."

"It doesn't matter to me. Maybe the garden? Zoe loves picking at the grass."

Marilyn ran back onto the porch and grabbed a blanket from the rocker. Cody swung the door open with his hip. A tray of glasses in his hand.

"Hey!" he called. "Welcome!"

Zoe greeted him with a squeal while I tried to play it cool by simply nodding in his direction. We followed Marilyn around to the expansive backyard. Beside the deck was an inground pool, surrounded by a white wooden gate. A large table and matching chairs with colorful cushions graced the deck. Huge painted clay pots stood along one side of the deck, the soil rich, brown, and bare.

Marilyn spread the blanket out as I plopped Zoe down on her bottom. She immediately flopped onto her tummy and scootched her way to the edge of the blanket, grabbing a handful of grass. I sat beside her while Marilyn and Cody joined me.

"I'm so glad you two could come for a visit." Marilyn passed out the lemonade. "Oh, I should ask you, do you want to us wear masks? We all got the Covid vaccine, but I want to make sure you and Zoe feel safe."

"I think we are okay, being outside and all." I took a gulp from the glass. "Thanks for the lemonade. Did you get really sick from the shot? I just signed up to get it, but I'm worried about being sick and having to take care of Zoe."

"It's better than getting Covid," Marilyn said. "It made me really tired for the rest of the day, but I was as right as rain the next morning. The boys got sick with fevers and such, but they were all better after about thirty-six hours."

Cody made it sound like the shot was a breeze. *36 hours?* I knew he got his shot, but then again, we'd only been chatting a few times a week at the time. Unlike now, where we had an ongoing dialogue all day long.

"Do you think that once everyone gets this shot, this will all be over?" I scooted over to lift Zoe back onto the blanket. She immediately pulled herself back onto the grass.

"Let's hope so." Marilyn sighed. "My husband, John, was adamant about not getting the vaccine. Started spouting all this nonsense about freedom and government. We let that ride for a while. Things got pretty tense. But a few weeks ago, his childhood friend got Covid and ended up passing away. He changed his mind after the funeral. Now I'm hearing about a second shot? I can't keep up. Things are always changing, but we certainly need to do everything we can to stop this thing."

"I'm sorry about your husband's friend."

We sat in silence for a moment, all three of us watching Zoe pushing herself up on all fours. I held my breath as she boldly eased her body forward, lifting her right arm to propel herself further into a crawl. I turned toward Marilyn and raised my eyebrows.

"Does that count as crawling?"

"You bet it does! I'd say you better start babyproofing. This little one is on the move."

She began to clap and cheer, and I joined in while Cody watched us make fools of ourselves.

"You did it Zoe!" I whooped.

"What a big girl!" Marilyn stood up and did a little dance while I lifted Zoe to my chest and swung her around. Cody's laughter filled the air, and a warmth filled my heart as we celebrated this milestone. *Is this what family feels like?*

****

To: Melaniewalker@catharsistimepress.com
From:Willowmorgan666@gmail.com
Subject: Age 16

Mel, It's been two months, and I haven't heard from you. Are you okay? I called the publishing company and spoke with Rose, who said you were taking a leave of absence. She told me you were still checking emails and to continue sending you whatever I had. My therapist thinks it's good for me to keep writing to you, even if I don't hear back. She talks a lot about trauma and 'parts resolution' and says that even if none of my stories are published, it's still therapeutic for me to process some of this stuff. The freelancing I do for work is an easy paycheck. Writing product reviews, editorial pieces, and even fiction is nothing compared to this. It pays the bills, which I'm grateful for. I know I'll never get rich, but as long as Zoe and I have food and a roof over our heads, that's all I need. Anyway, I hope you are okay and that I hear from you soon. -W

"The Lord will provide!" Mr. Calkins yelled from upstairs. Molly rolled her eyes as she looked at me. I pulled open the massive can of government peanut butter and poured some of the oil from the top of it into the sink. Stirring the rest into the can, I scolded myself for removing too much of the oil. Now the peanut butter was too dry. It crumbled a bit as I flaked it onto the celery before us. Molly plunked a few raisins onto each log, and I carried the plates into the living room.

"The Lord wants us to be good stewards and pay our bills, so we don't lose the house!" Mrs. Calkins shouted back.

Clicking on the TV, I turned up the volume, hoping to tune them out. I'd already read an hour of Bible passages out loud to Molly, so we could now enjoy some televised prairie adventures. Granted, I'd chosen racy passages from The Song of Solomon, but as long as it was from the Bible, we'd met the criteria of the "Bible Bank" rules. One hour of Bible for one hour of TV. Molly snuggled up to me on the couch, and I put my arm around her shoulder. I inched the volume up a bit more, hoping I wouldn't get in trouble.

A few months ago, Mr. Calkins lost his job again. He'd been laid off from his past three jobs. Now that Molly and I were the only remaining foster kids in the house, the money they were making off of us was tight. Dillon had been returned to his real family, and the twins had been adopted.

The Calkins always seemed to argue about money. Even before his rash of lost jobs, they fought about how to spend what little they had. Which bills could be paid this month? Pick and choose a bill, but always make sure you tithe ten percent to the church. Last week, Mr. C had made a donation to a famous religious organization after the televised fundraiser they had watched. This, of course, resulted in another big fight. Mrs. C screamed at him, while he went on and on about "good faith" and "God multiplying his money ten-fold" as the televangelist had promised.

A crash could be heard from upstairs, followed by Mrs. Calkins storming down the steps and slamming the door as she left. This was how it often played out. An argument about money, followed by lots of yelling and slamming things around, and her eventually screeching away in the car. I listened for the vroom of the ignition and the squeal of the tires. Instead, I heard an ungodly pounding on the door, followed by breaking glass. I froze, unsure of what to do. Molly stood and began to slowly walk toward the back door. I rushed past her, motioning for her to stay put. The TV blasted an awkward rendition of "Bringing in the Sheaves" in the background. The only other sound was Mrs. Calkin's sobbing.

As I approached the entryway, it was apparent the window there was broken. Mrs. Calkin's stood outside, holding her arm and crying.

"Go get Mr. C," I instructed. Molly's eyes grew wide, but she scampered up the stairs.

I ran into the kitchen and grabbed a towel. As I made my way back to the door, I could hear Mr. C's footsteps. Pulling open the door caused more glass to fall from the window. Mrs. C took a step back as I handed her the towel.

"What are you doing?" Mr. C pushed past me. "What happened?" He took the towel from his wife as she held out her bloody arm. A large gash tore the skin between her elbow and wrist.

"I forgot my keys." she winced as he wrapped her arm with the towel. "I was knocking on the door, and the glass broke. Didn't you hear me knocking? Why didn't anyone come to let me in?"

Molly's tiny hand slipped into mine, and I turned to look at her. Her face was tear-stained, and her eyes full of fear.

"This is going to need stitches." Mr. C turned to me. "Take care of Molly. I'm going to take her to the hospital for some stitches. We might be gone for a few hours. Can you grab the car keys for me?" I nodded and reached for the keys hanging on the hook nearby.

Mr. C turned back as he led his wife to the car. "And clean up the glass, will you?"

Molly and I watched them drive away. She grabbed the broom and began to sweep.

"It's okay. I'll do it in a bit. Let's go back and finish watching the show."

I followed her back into the living room. The house was finally peaceful as I breathed a sigh of relief.

Chapter Twenty-One

August 18, 2020

My insides were being ripped open. As a tight band of bright pain squeezed around my middle, another gush of amniotic fluid seeped down my legs. The clear trickle had soaked through my white nightgown, which now clung to me like a wet, deflated balloon. I lowered myself into the copper tub, which was barely large enough to contain my bloated body. I'd plugged my cellphone into the charger in the living room earlier. Although it was only in the next room, the idea of trying to stand and lift my foot over the mere twenty-eight-inch wall of the tub felt insurmountable.

My back rubbed angrily against the side of the tub as I tucked my nightgown up under my breasts. *I need to call Marilyn. I need help!* Marilyn had stopped by to check on me just two days ago. She said everything looked good. I certainly hadn't been in labor.

I can't do this! Not by myself! An inky blackness spread through my brain, pushing out any remaining thoughts as I held my breath while another wave of agony washed over me. It was as if the devil himself had his fiery talons around me and was ripping me apart.

"Noooo." I heard myself hiss in a voice that must have belonged to my mother. It was a sound I didn't recognize, and I felt myself morphing into another version of me. It had happened a few times before, as part of me slid away up toward the ceiling, and I watched this other me now in labor. The laboring me looked up as the sun peeked through the octagon window above the composting toilet. I'd hung a crystal from the wood frame, and prisms of rainbows flitted about the small space. I studied one, imagining myself inside all of the beautiful colors. Slowing my breath and willing myself to brace for more pain. Neither version of myself felt capable of bringing this baby into the world.

Why is this happening so fast? I need to get to my phone and call for help! My brain screamed, but my body protested at the thought of standing up.

Time faded away as I grunted and swore and cried in my little makeshift tub. And when he finally slid into this world, everything grew silent. I held his still, gray body in my lap. His eyes were closed. A swirl of black hair atop his head. A pool of blood beneath us.

Maybe if I cut the umbilical cord, then he will start to breathe? I scanned the bathroom. The nearest pair of scissors were tucked away on a shelf behind the mirror above the sink. Looking down at his lifeless body, I lifted him to my face to study him. His skin was caked with muck. I tipped my ear down to listen for breath, even though I already knew there was none. Reaching for the razor I'd left on the soap dish by the faucet, I flipped it over and wiggled the small knob to release the catch and allow the blade to fall into the soap dish. Carefully I picked it up and began to slice through the thick rubbery cord, watching for signs of life. When I'd fully freed him from my body, I felt around for the bathmat on the floor and pulled it into the tub with us. Laying him down on the fluffy whiteness, I could see how gray he really was. I bent and placed my mouth over his, covering his small nose with my lips. I blew a few puffs of air, pulling away to see if his chest would rise. My tears poured over his tiny face, washing away some of the sticky substance that clung to him. I don't know how much time passed before I gave up and drifted from the ceiling back into my body. A hot trickle of blood seeped from me into the cold, hard tub. A gush of pain snapped me from my haze.

****

June 24, 2021

"What's wrong?" Cody approached me cautiously. *How long have I been sitting here?* I wiped my eyes and focused my gaze back on to the rose bush before me. Zoe must be inside sleeping. The baby monitor he'd purchased for us peeked out of his pocket. He must have grabbed it while I was sitting here in a time-lapsed stupor. These episodes of time distortion happened more often than I'd like to admit. I couldn't even remember coming outside. *Am I in a dream, a memory or reality?* Knowing the difference was becoming increasingly difficult.

"Are you okay?" He squatted down beside me, eventually sitting on the warm earth. I must have come out to prune the rose bushes, even though I actually had no idea what I was doing or even what time of year I was supposed to prune them. The shears and watering can sit untouched nearby. Was it my imagination, or was the bush in the middle lusher than the others?

"Willow? What's going on? This is the second time I've found you out here crying."

I looked up at his beautiful face. It was full of innocence and love. *Love you don't deserve. You couldn't save your own baby, and you claimed another as your own. You don't deserve love. You're living a lie.* My shoulders ached with the weight of my silence. My head throbbed as I swallowed down my truth. I shook my head and offered him a small smile.

"I'm okay. Just tired, I guess."

He eyed me warily. As he reached for my hand, I began to cry again. His tender touch of love seemed to burn my skin. I pulled away, but the pain snaked its way into my core, causing more tears to flow.

Cody spoke quietly. "When I was little, I found my mom crying in the bathroom once. She was staring at herself in the mirror, crying. I think I was maybe four or five, and I couldn't remember seeing her cry before that. When I asked her what was wrong, she told me, 'Cody, sometimes people have an ache in their heart, and they don't know why.' Her words always stuck with me." He wrapped an arm around me, and I let him pull me closer.

"Do you have an ache in your heart?" His voice was low and warm.

I thought about telling him. About how freeing it would feel to admit to what I had done. The secret was weighing on me heavily. But then reality hit. If I told, I could lose Zoe. That was not a risk I was willing to take. I'd need to learn how to compartmentalize better. How to bury the secret deeper as I kept creating my new reality. Maybe I could keep getting away with it. Cody knew some of my darkness, and it hadn't scared him away yet. But this was too dark. It was a burden I had to carry alone.

"Let's go back inside. I'm thirsty." Shifting my weight, I started to stand, but Cody pulled me back down over to the grass.

"Is this about Molly?"

I flinched at the mention of her name. Why did talking about my past hurt so much? Why did I pride myself in doling out only a handful of truths about where I came from? It felt almost like a power I possessed. The power of closing myself off from the world. Tucking away the parts of me that felt raw and exposed. Because if people see how broken I really am, they might not like me. They might leave. He might leave.

That was a secret I'd finally given away. I've known him now for nearly a year. We'd been seriously dating for a few months now. Cody knew a bit about my childhood and about Molly. Whenever he'd asked me about her, I'd told him stories from when we were little. It wasn't until recently that I'd finally told him the rest of the story.

****

To: Melaniewalker@catharsistimepress.com
From:Willowmorgan666@gmail.com
Subject: Age 18
Mel, Are you reading this? Does it matter? -W

"I'll be okay." Molly folded my favorite shirt and placed it on the pile of clothes in my suitcase. The floral suitcase had been a birthday gift from the Calkins. Today I turned eighteen. Today I moved out.

"I know you will," I lied. Although she was nearly fifteen, Molly looked more like a twelve year old. Her dark, wild hair was pulled up into messy pigtails. Curls springing out around her oversized glasses gave her the appearance of a much younger child.

"I'd take you with me if I could."

Her chin quivered slightly, and she nodded. "I know."

I pulled the shirt off of the top of the pile. It was a soft, cotton tie-dyed shirt I'd made in school. The pink, blue and purple swirls made me feel bright and happy.

"You keep it." I handed it to her.

"No. I can't. It's your favorite, Willow." She tried to give it back to me.

"I want you to. Besides, in two and a half years, I'll have my own place, and you'll be eighteen and can move in with me. We can make loads more." I knew I had to hurry up. Angel was waiting outside in the car to take me to a small group home for girls transitioning out of foster care and trying to become independent. The Calkins had made it clear with each of their foster kids that their generosity only lasted until the checks stopped coming. They'd picked up another stray, this time a fifteen-year-old boy they doted on. Molly and I didn't like him. In fact, we avoided Stan as much as possible. Molly even started locking our bedroom door at night, convinced he was coming in and watching us sleep.

After losing the house to bankruptcy a few years back, we'd moved into a three-bedroom apartment on the other side of town. The apartment was one of the perks of the jobs they'd both landed as new apartment managers. Molly would now have a room to herself.

I worried for her. Although she had some friends at the tiny church school, she was quite secluded. She was too young to get a job, and when she wasn't forced to go to school, church, or clean up the apartment, she spent most of her time in bed. She often woke up crying in the middle of the night. The past few weeks had gotten worse, and I would regularly climb into bed to comfort her. Her small frame would tuck into mine as if willing herself to disappear. And she was disappearing. Each day she ate less and less. The extra small T-shirt I'd given her looked more like a huge dress on her. Several months ago, I'd finally worked up the nerve to ask Mrs. C for help.

"Molly is sick," I'd told her.

"Sick how?" She'd looked up from her devotion, annoyed at the intrusion.

"I think she's depressed. And she's not eating enough. Or sleeping. She needs help."

"She's fine. What she needs is to pray. She has nothing to be depressed about. She has a place to live and plenty of food to eat."

I was getting nowhere. I'd tried to get Molly to talk to the counselor at school. And when she finally did, they prayed with her and sent her on her way. They'd followed up with a call to the Calkins, who assigned *healing* scripture verses to Molly to read.

"Thank you," Molly said in a small voice. Lifting the shirt over her head and tugging it down over her. She looked like a tiny girl playing dress-up.

I pulled her into a bear hug, afraid I would crush her with my love.

"I'll text you when I get there." Although I would be staying less than an hour away, it felt like I was moving to another country. My heart squeezed tight as tears streamed down my face.

"I'll take the bus to come see you on the weekend." Letting go of her, I watched as she wiped her eyes with her bare arm, leaving a trail of snot on her skin. I turned back to her as I made my way toward the door.

"I love you, Molly. I'll be back for you." Tears clouded my vision as I left her behind.

Chapter Twenty-Two

July 17, 2021

When I woke, Cody was gone. He'd taken to staying over several nights a week, and last night we had binge-watched another Canadian comedy , so we'd turned in late. Zoe slept in her crib under the alcove beneath the stairs. I could hear her from anywhere in the house, but I kept a small video monitor Cody brought us on the shelf beside the bed anyway. I studied it for any sign of movement. She was still asleep. The house was quiet.

Stretching out in the bed and wiggling my toes, I enjoyed the softness of the jersey knit sheets. Growing up, my sheets always seemed to be scratchy and ill-fitting. The sides often popped off and rolled toward me as I slept. My job as a freelance writer didn't pay a lot, but I was able to cover my expenses, and I'd invested in two pairs of extra soft sheets. A set of flannel for the winter and jersey cotton for the summer. *Why did he leave so early?* The familiar buzz in my brain began the loop of worries.

Maybe he's not interested anymore. Maybe I'm not happy enough for him. I should probably increase my antidepressant. I'm too much. Too angry. Too dark. My OCD must bother him. I don't touch him enough. I don't hide the fact I don't always want to be touched.

Can he tell how much I think of germs every time he reaches for me?

What if he doesn't really want to be in a relationship with a single mom?

What if he can't handle my level of crazy?

A bloom of bright red blood filled the space alongside the cuticle of my thumb. I hadn't even noticed I'd been picking it until it started to bleed. I grabbed a tissue from the side table and sat up. Pressing the softness to my throbbing skin.

What if he found out about Zoe? What if he dug around near the rose bushes and found the evidence of Charles? I started to cry. Great sobs began to wrack my body, releasing more of the pent-up sadness I tried so hard to hold down. I'd been crying a lot lately. I'd always cried way too easily. When I turned twenty, I finally asked my doctor for an antidepressant to take the edge off. It helped a bit but didn't leave me as emotionally numb as I wanted to be and added another ten pounds to my already curvy-in-the-wrong-places frame.

What if...What if...What if... My brain was once again stuck in loop mode. It happened more than I'd like to admit. I'd once gone to a therapist who diagnosed me with *Pure O*, some kind of knockoff of Obsessive-Compulsive Disorder. I was cursed with obsessive and repetitive thoughts...germs...people's names...mistakes I'd made...people who had hurt me...people I'd lost along the way....

The thoughts were never too far away. Sometimes I'd wake up, and the loop would begin immediately. On a good day, I could distract myself with Zoe or cleaning the house, or gardening. But the thoughts would always return. Sometimes the loop was a good one. *Cody. Cody. Cody.* Last week I woke up with his name on repeat in my mind. It was a morning he wasn't here, and I guess I must have missed his presence. *Cody, Cody, Cody. Where is he?*

Zoe stirred and began to babble. Her singsong noises breaking the spell. I tugged on a clean shirt and shorts and took the four steps from the loft to the landing. She sounded happy, so I flipped on the coffee maker and I passed through the kitchen, ducking into the bathroom.

Someday I'd like to live off-grid, with solar power and a fully sustainable home. But I wasn't brave enough, and I didn't have much left in savings to even begin to think of that as an option. I washed my hands twice while studying myself in the round mirror above my copper sink. My eyes were ringed with red from crying. My dingy hair hung loose and limp. I grabbed the hairband from my wrist and pulled it into a messy bun. Then I washed my hands again. For good measure.

Zoe was blowing raspberries and singing nonsense words as I went over to get her. She'd pulled herself up and was standing holding onto the bars of the crib.

"Well, look at you!"

She grinned and signed she was ready to be picked up.

"Hungry?" I asked her.

She signed she wanted milk.

I backed into the kitchen propping her on my hip as I pulled the formula out of the cupboard. Sensing movement from outside, I froze for a moment and leaned forward to look out the picture window. Nothing. I carried Zoe through the living room to the window in the top of the dutch door. It was Cody. Breathing a sigh of relief, I unlocked the door and pulled the top half open. Setting Zoe on the ledge, I let her dangle her tiny legs outside as I held her middle tightly. My head aligned with hers.

"Look at you two fine ladies," Cody called as he made his way onto the step. He was carrying one of my reusable shopping bags on one shoulder.

"You went shopping?" I peeked my head out from behind Zoe's, and he leaned forward to kiss my cheek. I tried to ignore the wetness of the germs he left behind. Zoe squealed and reached for him.

"Did you use hand sanitizer?" I felt shame creep from the pit of my stomach up to my chest as I said the words. I knew it was annoying, but I didn't want him to pass anything on to Zoe.

"I did. At the checkout." His dimple disappeared. "But I'll do it again." He set the bag down on the step, and I handed him the pump of hand sanitizer I kept just inside the door. After a generous squirt and vigorous rubbing, I let go of Zoe, and he pulled her to him.

I pushed the lower half of the door open and stepped outside. The warmth of the day felt luscious against my skin.

"What'd ya get?" I eyed the bag with curiosity.

"Well," he began, handing Zoe back to me. "For starters, I got you a blueberry muffin."

"Oh god, I love you." The words fell out of my mouth before I could stop them. *Love, love, love. You said it.* My brain screamed. I'd simply meant I loved the gesture of kindness for the muffin. He grinned at me, his dimple reappearing as he held the muffin at arm's length.

"What was that?" he teased. "You *love* me?" We both knew it to be true. He'd told me he loved me nearly two weeks ago, and I hadn't said it back yet.

I felt cracked open inside. Raw and weak. Like a baby bird reliant on her mother for survival. I didn't want to be reliant on anyone but myself.

I took Zoe back from him and plopped down on the front step. I stared at the top of her silky head as I settled her onto my lap. The sunlight made her hair look more red than blonde. He handed me the muffin with a small smile.

"I knew it," he whispered. "Does it feel scary?" His voice grew quieter as she scooted his body next to mine on the step. Our hips touched, and Zoe careened her body toward his lap. He took her back, and I suddenly missed the warmth of her tiny body shielding me.

I gave him a slight nod. Not wanting to take back the words. I let them circulate in the sultry breeze as I took a bite of the muffin.

****

July 2021

"Long Haul Covid, that's what the doctor said." Aubrey looked stressed as I watched her from my laptop screen. Her eyes were tired. Maybe it was the lighting, but I swear she had a wrinkle between her brows. *Are we supposed to start using wrinkle cream before we even hit thirty?* I tilted my computer so I could finish making myself a cup of tea while we chatted.

"Geez, Aub. That sucks. I'm sorry. I read something about Long Covid, or whatever they are calling it. It sounds awful."

I carried my mug and laptop to the couch and

balanced my device on my lap while I took a long sip.

"How are you drinking hot tea right now? Isn't it like ninety degrees out or something?" Aubrey took a sip of her ice water, the glass clinking as she moved it closer to her.

"It's eighty-seven, and I like tea in the morning. It's soothing."

"It's hot," she reminded me as if I'd forgotten. Cody had taken Zoe for a walk to visit his mom, so I could call to check on Aubrey and Brian. We'd been invited for dinner with his family, and I'd told him I'd walk over after the call.

"Has he been able to go back to work?" I broached the subject lightly, knowing Aubrey was worried about money. They'd been lucky enough to be able to work mostly from home, but he was the primary breadwinner.

"He's working a few hours from home every day. They've been really understanding so far. He just gets super tired so easily." She pulled the camera closer and whispered. "He's driving me a bit nuts."

"What do you mean?" As much as I wanted her to, Aubrey rarely complained about Brian.

"I feel bad. I mean, I know he's tired and all, but I wish he'd just leave the house a bit. Even if he just went for a short walk. Give me some space."

I nodded. Needing space was something I understood well. The arrangement Cody and I had so far was working well. He stayed over three nights a week. The rest of the time, it was just me and Zoe. Lately, he'd been hinting at moving in. This terrified me, and every time he'd broached the subject, I'd managed to move the conversation in a different direction.

"Maybe you could get out more? Do some gardening or something?"

"I hate gardening. You know that. I have the black thumb of death. But you're right. I should get out more." She raised her eyebrows and grinned menacingly.

"What is *that* look for?" I mimicked her expression..

"Well…not to invite myself to your place, but maybe I could take a day trip to see you and Zoe." She paused. "And meet Cody?"

"Ahh, there it is." I knew she was up to something. Ever since I finally told her about Cody, she's been relentless in her questions.

"First of all, you are *always* welcome here. There is a standing invitation. Secondly," I paused, wracking my brain for reasons why she shouldn't meet him. He was by far the best person I'd ever dated and the most serious relationship I'd had so far. She waited for me to continue.

"I guess there is no second. You are welcome anytime."

"Yay!' She squealed. Eve suddenly appeared and jumped onto her lap. "I'm okay, Eve. Shh. What about Zoe's birthday? Are you having a party? Would it be too chaotic if I come for the day?"

"What a great idea. I mean, with Covid and all, we weren't planning much. Just some cake, maybe a trip to the beach."

"*We.*" She stretched out the word with an extra wide grin. "You said *we*, as in you and Cody, are planning it together? That's so cute!" she gushed.

The heat rose to my cheeks as I returned my cup of tea to the table. Maybe I should switch to something cooler.

Chapter Twenty-Three

To: Melaniewalker@catharsistimepress.com
From:Willowmorgan666@gmail.com
Subject: Age 21
Mel, I'm out of words. -W

The nagging feeling of dread settling along my spine was telling me something. I should have started listening when I woke up that morning. Instead, I got ready for work and stood at the bus stop waiting to spend the day with a room full of three-year-olds at the daycare that had just hired me. Angel had found me a job, and although I'd only worked there now for two weeks, I'd already fallen in love with it. Three-year-olds are beyond exhausting. But they love with a ferocity I admired and, needless to say, soaked up. Each day I returned to my shared room tired and sore. My roommate Cheryl was rarely there as she spent most of her nights sleeping at the firehall she volunteered for, so I was able to flip on the tiny TV that Angel had found for me and eat my soup noodles in my fold-out bed.

I should have known from the moment I opened my eyes that morning that something was wrong. Apparently, I'd unknowingly pressed snooze too many times, so the emergency backup alarm clock I'd set up across the room blared, forcing me to climb out of bed and turn it off.

Disoriented and bleary-eyed, I stumped across the

cold floor and smashed the button into oblivion.

"Shut the fuck up!" was followed by a pounding on the wall behind me. Apparently my neighbors weren't early risers.

Sighing, I pulled open my plastic bin and shook out the T-shirt on the top of the pile. It was wrinkled, but it would have to do. I had ten minutes to get to the bus stop, which luckily was right at the corner. I grabbed my backpack, shoved a few granola bars and a juice box in it, and paused in the hallway to see if the communal bathroom was occupied. The door was open, so I ran in there to do my business as quickly as possible. I washed my hands two extra times, hoping it would soothe the nagging worry that tugged at my chest.

My burner phone chirped from the front pocket of my bag, but I ignored it and ran to the bus stop. Once there, I pulled out my phone and flipped it open. There were three voicemails from Molly.

I listened to the first message as I took my seat on the bus.

"Willow, I just want you to know I love you," she said in a small voice. The line went dead, and I pulled the phone away from my face to check the timestamp. *3:37 a.m.* Strange. Molly had left me cryptic messages before. I suspected she was drinking or taking something that loosened her tongue. I'd gotten several voicemail messages from her over the past few weeks where she reminded me that she loved me.

Last week she left a rambling voicemail, her words tumbling over each other to reach my ear. Her eighteenth birthday was next month, and she couldn't wait to move out of the Calkins' house and in with me.

Angel had placed her on the waiting list for the home I was staying at, but since there wasn't an opening, we didn't know where she was going to live yet. I'd already managed to save most of my paychecks, but I wasn't anywhere near close enough to saving enough for a deposit for an apartment, much less rent on a monthly basis.

The second voicemail was sent seventeen minutes later. Molly's voice sounded as if she'd been crying.

"I'm sorry, Willow. I tried so hard. But I can't do it anymore." I bolted upright in my seat. How close was I to the next stop? Maybe I could transfer buses and head over to the Calkins to check on her.

"Don't worry about me," she continued. Her words were slurring and slow. "I feel good now. I'm gonna be h-happy. Remember the roads are pa-paved in go-ld? It's gonna be so pretty."

Frantically, I made my way down the aisle toward the driver. My backpack bumped into the side of the seat beside me as the bus turned a corner. I held the phone to my ear as I shouted to the driver.

"I need to get off. It's an emergency."

She pulled up to the corner and flicked her lights on. The door swished open as I stepped back out into the bright morning. Where am I? What should I do? That was the end of the voicemail. Do I dare listen to the next one? My heart already knew what my brain couldn't accept. I sank down onto the gritty pavement, ignoring the men standing at the corner staring at me. Dazed, I lifted the phone back to my ear to listen to the final message. It was nineteen seconds of deafening silence. My heart raced as tears streamed down my face. *No! No! No! She's okay. It's not what you think it is.*

My fingers felt as heavy as lead as I dialed the Calkins number. No one picked up. I hung up and dialed again. Nothing. I dialed Angel, and she picked up on the third ring.

"Willow? What's wrong?" I could hear country music playing in the background. Was she in her car?

"It's Molly. Something's wrong. She left me these voicemails…and I don't know what to think." I sobbed. Tears clouded my vision. Snot ran down into my mouth.

"Where are you? Are you at work?" The music faded.

I looked up at the street sign. I had no idea where I was or where I should be.

"Um. Hold on." I squinted into the sun. "I'm on the corner of Main and Grape. By this store. Um, Shelby's?"

"Geez, Willow. Hold on. Are you safe? Stay where you are. I'll be there soon. Okay?"

I nodded as if she could hear me. Staring at my phone, I held my breath as I dialed Molly's number. Nothing. No answer.

I tried the Calkins' number again. This time, someone picked up.

"Hello?" It was Mr. Calkins. It was the only time I was ever glad to hear his gravelly voice.

"Mr. C. It's Willow. Is Molly there? Is she okay? Can you check on her? She left me these messages, and I'm worried…" He cut me off.

"Willow? What are you talking about?" Mr. Calkins cleared his throat. "Molly stayed overnight at the church. She isn't here. Last night was the youth group lock-in. She's probably still there. I dropped her off last night."

"Somethings wrong!" I shouted into the phone. "Are you sure she went? Can you check her room?"

"Stop yelling. Okay, I'll check."

I could hear him walking up the steps to our room. The creak of the door. Then silence. His voice soft in my ear. "She's not here. I need to go pick her up from church soon, though. Do you want me to have her call you?"

I wanted to be wrong. I wanted to be wrong with my whole heart. The words stuck in my throat as I pushed them out with a sob.

"Did she leave anything for me?"

"What? What are you talking about? Listen, Willow. I'm sure she's fine. I'm picking her up soon. Pastor Mettin said to pick up the kids at eleven.

"Did she leave anything for me?" I yelled into the phone. The men outside the store eyed me warily.

"The only thing here is a T-shirt. A folded tie dye, shirt. It's on her bed. Is that what you mean?"

My stomach seized up, and I bent over, trying to alleviate the pain.

"You have to go to church now. Find her. Something is wrong." It was the boldest I'd ever dared to be with him.

Angel's car screeched up to the curb. I watched her sneakers thump toward me. The cracked nylon faded from my view as I slumped over, my phone clacking to the ground.

****

August 2021

Sunlight kissed Zoe's hair as she grabbed fistfuls

of sand. I glanced at the clusters of families spread across the beach. Most people were maskless, but a few faces remained covered. *Will life ever return to normal?* Aubrey spread her towel out a few feet from mine and sighed.

"It's nice here. Thanks again for having me."

"I'm glad you could come, even if you can only stay for the day."

Since Zoe was the only one among us who couldn't get vaccinated yet, I was still nervous she could get sick. I'd heard of many people who were getting Covid even after lining up to get a shot. The news was now droning on about multiple doses of the vaccine. Politics clouded judgments, and I was sick of the whole thing. For now, we continued to limit our contact with the rest of the world.

"Cody is amazing." Aubrey looked over at him as he sprinkled sand on Zoe's chubby legs. "I'm so happy you found each other."

If he stays. The thought was on a loop in my brain that played on a regular basis. It was as if I couldn't fully allow myself to free fall, engulfed by his love. I was always waiting for something bad to happen. Every time he left to go back home, or even to run to the store, bracing against complete abandonment. The steely fear of loss was never far. And it wasn't just selective to him. Each time I put Zoe down for a nap, I prayed she would wake back up again. I checked her sleeping form for breath multiple times as she dozed. *Do other people live this way? Unable to fully live because death and disaster were just around the corner, ready to snatch everything away in an unexpected instant?*

I shook the thoughts away momentarily and stood

to stretch in the sun.

"Do you want to go in the water? I'm gonna dip Zoe's feet in." I glanced down back at Aubrey, who shook her head and waved me on. Catching Cody's gaze, I watched him traipse over toward us and scoop Zoe up. She squealed in glee.

"Wanna go in?"

I nodded. The three of us looked at Aubrey, who chuckled and gave an exaggerated sigh. "Oh, all right. But it better not be freezing cold!"

The water was perfect as we waded to our waists. Cody carefully passed Zoe to me. I held her tightly as she kicked her feet.

"Wa. O-ooWa. Oowa." she said.

I nearly dropped her in surprise.

"Oowa." she repeated as her tiny feet pumped the water.

"I think she's trying to say 'water!'"

Cody and Aubrey moved closer to us, but Zoe merely kicked her feet silently. I tried willing her to speak again.

"That's great!" Cody wrapped his arms around my waist and drew Zoe and me close to him.

"My girls," he murmured in my ear as I pushed the loop of fear as far from my brain as possible.

****

By the time we reached the church, I was in full-blown panic mode. Angel made me hold a cold bottle of water against my forehead during the drive, and despite her best efforts of calming me down, I was a mess.

I flung open the door as she pulled up to the bus loop by the church. The doors were usually unlocked, so I headed for the main door leading to the school. I prayed to a God I no longer believed in, that I was wrong, and Molly was safe. Pastor Mettin stood in front of the door leading to the gymnasium where the lockdown event was being held.

"Hold on, Willow." He motioned for me to step back. Angel had called the church on the way over, and the secretary must have alerted him we were looking for Molly.

"There's no reason to upset any of the kids here. Molly is probably fine. We haven't located her yet, but it's possible she left last night without us knowing."

"Last night?" I shouted at him. Angel placed a heavy hand on my elbow. "You haven't seen her since last night? Did someone think to check on her? Did anyone even call the Calkins?"

"You know she's left in the middle of youth group before, right?" The pastor's seemed nonplussed. "I don't see what the big deal is."

I pushed past him and scoured the gym for any sight of her.

"Have any of you seen Molly?" I shouted over the din of conversation as a few of the remaining kids wandered over.

A freakishly tall boy answered. "She left last night. I think she decided she didn't want to stay over. Maybe she went home?" He slung his faded backpack over his shoulder.

"Did you tell anyone she left?"

He shrugged.

I pushed past the lingering onlookers and headed into the small chapel attached to the gym. It was empty. Breathing in the scent of polished pews and moldy

Bibles, I made my way through the oppressive space and into the hallway leading to the sanctuary and nursery. Suddenly, I knew where she was.

The bottom of the Dutch door to the nursery was latched. I reached over the top of the mahogany and lifted the mechanism to swing it open. The wall of empty cribs looked ominous as I pushed open the door to the back room and rounded the bend. My heart sank as tears clouded my vision. Her impossibly tiny body sat slumped in the corner.

"Molly! No…no…no." I felt someone grab my arm, and I yanked it away. Angel appeared and squatted down beside her. I sank to the floor, pushing aside Molly's bag and several empty pill bottles.

"Molly?" She gently probed her neck for a pulse. "Someone call an ambulance!" She yelled back at the small crowd of slack-jawed onlookers now congregating in the doorway. One teen gave me a thumbs up as she held a phone to her ear. A few of them began to pray. Whispered pleas soon became chants of desperation. Pastor Mettin began to speak in tongues.

But his babbling never reached the heavens.

Lowering my head onto her cold chest, I listened for any sign of life. She was impossibly still. Her shirt was now damp from my tears. I clung to her and sobbed. I cried for the life we wouldn't get to share. I cried for the years of pain she carried. The hollow space in my heart grew deeper and deeper until someone pulled me away from her and guided me to the rocking chair. This room, this space that used to bring me such comfort, was now a plush chamber of death. The throng of sinners praying in the distance.

Cursing any semblance of "God" that might linger in these walls, I vowed to never set foot in a church again.

Chapter Twenty-Four

August 2021

Zoe's laughter filled the air as Aubrey swung her in a circle.

"I dunno, Willow. I never thought I would want kids, but she is awfully cute." She planted a kiss on Zoe's cheek and handed her back to me.

"She is the cutest baby in the world. But I'm biased," I replied. Zoe signed to be let down, and I bent, placing her feet in the grass as her tiny fingers grasped mine. She'd recently started toddling while we held her hands. Her grasp on me is slightly lighter each day.

"I'll miss you guys. Thanks for the visit. I'd better hit the road, though." Aubrey opened her car door and tossed her bag inside.

"Thanks for coming for her birthday. It meant a lot to us. Come visit anytime. Maybe Brian will be up to coming next time? Speaking of which, are you ready to change your mind about having babies?" Aubrey had been dead set against having kids since she was a little girl.

She shrugged and gave me a tiny grin.. "I dunno. I've been thinking about it for a while. And even though Brian says he's okay with whatever I want, I know he wants to start a family. We'll see. We've still got a lot of stuff to work out."

I wanted to ask her more but knew she had to go. It was a topic I would definitely bring up later. Now that she knew about Cody, she opened up more about her and Brian and their *friends*. It was a world both foreign and fascinating to me and I loved the way they all seemed to navigate this complicated type of love. Scooping Zoe back up, I waited until Aubrey got into her car and rolled down the window.

"Say goodbye to Auntie Bree." I tipped Zoe down to the window and raised her hand in a wave. "Text me when you get home."

"Will do! Bye guys!" She backed out, and we watched her drive away. My phone buzzed from my back pocket, and I pulled it out and glanced at the screen.

—*Do you girls wanna meet me for ice cream?*— Cody attached a gif of a cartoon bear licking a colorful ice cream cone to his text.

"It's only eleven a.m." I wrote back.

I let go of one of Zoe's hands, and she gripped my fingers as she waddled along the side of the house with me. I could almost see the sunny aura of happiness emanating from my daughter.

"Okay," I replied.

****

The fever started in the middle of the night. I woke drenched in sweat and kicked the tangled sheets from my legs.

"What's wrong?" Cody turned over and flung an arm across my chest. Irritated, I pushed him aside and sat up in bed. Blinking, I tried to reorient myself. My brain felt cobwebby. My eyes burned. Was I still asleep? I stared down at my arms. I could still feel the weight of my dead baby boy cradled there. *It was a dream. He's gone.* I reminded myself. Pushing away the thought as I pictured Zoe's face in my mind.

"I have to check on Zoe," I mumbled.

"What? Why?" Cody felt for his phone on the nightstand and flipped it over. "It's not even six o'clock." Placing a cool hand on my forehead, he pulled back in alarm.

"Geez, Willow. You're burning up. You have a fever. Let me get you some ibuprofen." He disappeared, tiptoeing down the stairs. I could hear him rummaging through my tiny medicine cabinet. He returned a minute later with two tablets and a glass of water.

I dutifully swallowed them down and tried to find a comfortable position. Zoe would be awake in an hour. I'd never tried to take care of her while feeling so sick.

"Go back to sleep, babe. I'll take care of Zoe," Cody whispered as if reading my mind. I tossed and turned. My spine ached, and my head throbbed, but eventually, I dozed off. A fever dream of truth too over my consciousness.

****

July 29, 2020
Birth

Damp soil crusted my fingernails as I patted down the earth in front of my rose bush. I thought I knew what pain was before now, but I didn't have a clue. A cavern of anguish seemed to surround me. Fatigue and sorrow weighed me down like an anchor. A sense of urgency crept down my spine as I pulled myself back up. *Go back inside! Hurry*! My thoughts swirled around me in dark confusion. The edges of my mind felt black and fuzzy. Nothing made sense. Hadn't I just been in the house? How did I get out here? Was I imagining a baby crying? Where was it coming from? As if moving through a web of gelatin, I forced my legs to walk back to my house. Up the front step. Through the door. Each stride was heavy but resigned.

The shrill cry of my baby filled my ears. But wait, had he ever cried? Could I imagine a sound that I'd never heard? His still, lifeless form had emerged into a silent tomb. Was I delusional? My hands instinctively moved to my bloated belly as I followed the sound. Sliding the pocket door of the bathroom all the way open, I stood transfixed as I stared at the bottom of the tub. There, beside the pulpy, alien-like blob of placenta, lay a baby. A live baby.

I gasped and eased my way down beside the copper basin. The crying continued. This time I joined in. It made no sense. But there, amidst the muck and blood, was another baby. The umbilical cord had clearly been severed by my hand. The bloody razor edge still sat nearby. Was I the one who made this cut? Another version of me? My mind could not seem to make sense of the scene unfolding in front of me. Lifting the child, I scooted along the floor until I could reach the towel hanging on the peg beside the pedestal sink. Gently, I wiped her mottled, pink skin as the face as my daughter stared up at me.

I wrapped her in the bath towel and set her bundled form on the bathroom floor as I became aware of the trickle of blood creeping down my inner thigh. Grabbing a thick pad from the basket under the sink, I pulled out a clean pair of underwear and pajamas I'd kept there. I shoved the pad in place as I clumsily dressed. My body screamed in protest as I bent to scoop her up, and we made our way to the couch. We sank into the cushions as I lifted her to my breast, and she began to suckle. During my pregnancy, I'd read countless articles about the benefits of breastfeeding. My own mother, snatched away by the jaws of life, had been unable to provide me with that. I was determined to bond with this foreign child. The effort of keeping my gaze trained on her face became too much, and I began to doze.

When I woke, another version of myself emerged. How much time had passed? Hours? Days? I pulled myself up and began to wander my tiny house in a haze. Stopping in the bathroom, I stared at this face in the mirror.

Something was off. My eyes saw familiar but distorted face peering out from behind the glass. I turned and locked my sight on the dried blood on the bottom of the tub. A broken razor lay nearby. A bloody bath rug sat in a crumpled heap on the floor. Flashes of memories hit me, and I sat down on the closed lid of the toilet as I buried my face in my hands, trying to make sense of it all. My fingernails smell of damp earth. Had a child died? Did I bury him? Was it a delusion? Was it real? I swiped away hot, angry tears and pulled myself back up as I made my way to the front door and flung it open. Blinking into the harsh morning light, I froze and stared at the box in front of me. Was I dreaming? Looking down at my hands, I counted each finger…9…10…11? Perplexed, I dropped my hands and stepped forward.

Finding myself on my front step, I stared at the howling baby in a box. Who would do such a thing? Did I put her here? Glancing around, I saw no other sign of life. I lifted the child and carried her around to the back of the house. Her reverent silence matched mine as I stood facing the rose bush. The mound of soil in front of it was fresh. Part of me wanted to dig it back up. Part of me was too scared to do so. I knelt, pulling the warmth of her bundled body from me. I lay her on the mound of dirt. Silent, she stared up at me in wonder. Should I leave her here? Where did she come from? Was she meant to be mine? She began to cry.

"Shh baby. Shh. You're all right. We're gonna be all right."

****

November 2021

"You're not crazy." Dr. Thomas watched me from his chair as I shifted uncomfortably in mine. "People dissociate for all sorts of reasons. Usually, dissociation stems from childhood trauma, and we both know you've survived quite a lot of that."

I yanked another tissue from the box in my lap and swiped at my eyes. Globs of black mascara stuck to the softness, and I reprimanded myself for even wearing mascara to this appointment. I'd been putting it off, but Dr. Thomas had always been good to me. Even when I let years go by without calling on him, he always took me back. He helped me make sense of the absurd.

"So, you're saying that I imagined Zoe being put in the box? Then how did she end up there? Does that mean I imagined my son? Did I kill him? Did I bury him? How can you say I'm not crazy? Cuz, I certainly feel crazy." A sob-laugh escaped in spite of the tears coursing down my face.

"Willow, do you still have the box?"

I shook my head. "It was just a diaper box. I've

gone through dozens of them by now."

"Did Marilyn ever tell you that you were carrying twins during any of your exams?" I shook my head again.

"Did she ever mention another heartbeat?"

Again, no.

"Obviously, I wasn't there, so this is pure speculation on my part but isn't it possible," he paused to push the waste paper basket toward me with his designer leather shoe. "Isn't it possible that what you buried under the rosebush was the placenta?"

I gathered the pile of used tissues from my lap and plopped them into the basket. *That had never occurred to me.* All this time, I'd been carrying the weight of thinking I lost a child. I'd held on to the delusion that Zoe magically appeared in his place. Sometimes when you live with a delusion for long enough, it becomes your truth. Our narratives often change to match the stories in our heads, even if those stories are not grounded in reality.

Another dark thought popped into my head, causing a sob to escape. "Does this mean I have multiple personalities?"

"Are you referring to Dissociative Identity Disorder?"

I nodded, afraid of his answer.

"No," he reassured me. "But I do think you have had some dissociative episodes. Usually, they've happened during times in your life when you were under a huge amount of stress or dealing with a major trauma. You've mentioned a few things over the years that made me wonder if that was what was happening. It's possible you have been experiencing a type of postpartum psychosis as well. Is it something you feel like you'd like to keep exploring?"

His voice was kind, without a trace of judgment in it.

Again, I nodded and reached for another tissue.

Epilogue

To: Melaniewalker@catharsistimepress.com
From:Willowmorgan666@gmail.com
Subject: Age 29

Mel, are you real or a delusion? My therapist asked me to contemplate if your existence would change my story in any way. I guess my story would still belong to me no matter who reads it (or doesn't.) Looking back over the chapters of my life, there are still moments I don't fully understand. If I'm being honest, there are still some entire years I don't remember. Should I? Maybe I'm not meant to remember everything. Maybe that's okay. Either way, I guess I'll keep sending you these excerpts. I've saved them all on my laptop. Who knows? Maybe someday I'll compile them and turn them into a book. The story isn't finished yet. –W

****

Zoe twirled in her frilly frock. Its white edges already stained with green. Her bare feet caked with earth.

"Do you remember what to do?" I straightened the crown of roses on her head as she giggled and danced around.

"Walk straight. Throw flowers at people. Stand by Cody." She paused in her jig to pick up a few stray petals that had flown from her basket during her last twirl.

"Not *at* the people!" Aubrey giggled.. "Just throw them to the ground, right?

Zoe nodded, prancing around.

Aubrey gently lifted Zoe and plunked her on the path of white fabric we'd placed on the lawn, before returning to her seat. "Get ready," she whispered.

As the music started, I watched my daughter flit down the aisle. A few chairs lined each side. I caught Angel's gaze, and a burst of joy filled my heart. The seat beside her was empty except for the small folded tie-dyed T-shirt I'd placed there. Marilyn dabbed her eyes from the other side of the aisle. Cody's dad and siblings grinned at me as I made my way down the aisle to Cody. His dimple is deep and sincere. His eyes are full of love.

Aubrey and Brian sat nearby. A tall, bespectacled man sat next to Brian. Aubrey's grin was as expansive as her hair. Her baby bump was barely noticeable under her forest green dress. They looked happy.

Zoe danced over to me and slipped her hand in mine as I turned to look at the small group of family we'd created. I'd spent so much of my life guarding my heart, convinced that if I let someone get too close they were bound to hurt me. But we all need love. And no matter how hard we try to shield ourselves from it, we are going to get hurt. We can't choose the families we are born into. Our losses and traumas may shape up, but they don't have to define us. Maybe God isn't a giant deity only found in the church. Maybe God is something harder to define. A home, a friend, a child. Perhaps they each carry a whisper of God within them. Maybe it's our job to quiet ourselves enough to listen. To see.

"Go," the spirits that had left us too soon gently whispered in the wind. This was my church. This was my home. This was my God.

A note from the author…

Writing this book was a challenge. As with any creative work, there will be people who don't like it. Perhaps it will rub them the wrong way. Perhaps they will make the assumption that I am making fun of their beliefs, or of organized religion. I acknowledge that. And as a former chronic people pleaser, that makes me uncomfortable. If my writing elicits strong feelings within you, fosters empathy or encourages critical thinking while entertaining, I have done my job.

Religion can be used to bring people together. To build community. To create change. To worship, learn and thrive. Unfortunately, as the past few years have shown us, religion can also be used to divide, harm, abuse and accelerate political agendas. Regardless of what you believe, my wish is that we, as a collective society, can step back and view humanity through a wider lens. How refreshing it would be to set aside agendas and simply love each other. Shine the light that is within you, and look for that light in others. It's there.

A word about the author...

Creative outlets have always been therapeutic for me. As a young girl, I often escaped my reality through the adventures provided by a good book. Writing has also been cathartic, and although some of my writing contains elements of my own story, much of it also touches on stories that my clients have shared with me.

When I'm not writing, reading or performing on stage, I'm helping clients share their stories.

I currently work as a therapist and live with my husband, two children, two cats and free-range bunny in upstate NY.

https://www.facebook.com/ZavackiMooreChoosingCharity/about

https://wordpress.com/view/sarazavackimoore.wordpress.com

https://www.instagram.com/sarazmooretherapistauthor/

www.hypnohelpservices.com

Thank you for purchasing
this publication of The Wild Rose Press, Inc.

For questions or more information
contact us at
info@thewildrosepress.com.

The Wild Rose Press, Inc.
www.thewildrosepress.com